PRAISE FOR THE DCI RYAN MYSTERIES

What newspapers say

"She keeps company with the best mystery writers" – *The Times*

"LJ Ross is the queen of Kindle" – *Sunday Telegraph*

"*Holy Island* is a blockbuster" – *Daily Express*

"A literary phenomenon" – *Evening Chronicle*

"A pacey, enthralling read" – *Independent*

What readers say

"I couldn't put it down. I think the full series will cause a divorce, but it will be worth it."

"I gave this book 5 stars because there's no option for 100."

"Thank you, LJ Ross, for the best two hours of my life."

"This book has more twists than a demented corkscrew."

"Another masterpiece in the series. The DCI Ryan mysteries are superb, with very realistic characters and wonderful plots. They are a joy to read!"

Also by LJ Ross

THE DCI RYAN MYSTERIES

1. *Holy Island*
2. *Sycamore Gap*
3. *Heavenfield*
4. *Angel*
5. *High Force*
6. *Cragside*
7. *Dark Skies*
8. *Seven Bridges*
9. *The Hermitage*
10. *Longstone*
11. *The Infirmary (Prequel)*
12. *The Moor*
13. *Penshaw*
14. *Borderlands*
15. *Ryan's Christmas*
16. *The Shrine*
17. *Cuthbert's Way*
18. *The Rock*
19. *Bamburgh*
20. *Lady's Well*
21. *Death Rocks*
22. *Poison Garden*
23. *Belsay*
24. *Berwick*

THE ALEXANDER GREGORY THRILLERS

1. *Impostor*
2. *Hysteria*
3. *Bedlam*
4. *Mania*
5. *Panic*
6. *Amnesia*
7. *Obsession*

THE SUMMER SUSPENSE MYSTERIES

1. *The Cove*
2. *The Creek*
3. *The Bay*
4. *The Haven*

DEATH ROCKS

A DCI RYAN MYSTERY

DEATH ROCKS

A DCI RYAN MYSTERY

LJ ROSS

PENGUIN BOOKS

PENGUIN BOOKS

UK | USA | Canada | Ireland | Australia
India | New Zealand | South Africa

Penguin Books is part of the Penguin Random House group of companies
whose addresses can be found at global.penguinrandomhouse.com

Penguin Random House UK,
One Embassy Gardens, 8 Viaduct Gardens, London SW11 7BW

penguin.co.uk

First published by LJ Ross 2024
Published in Penguin Books 2026
001

Copyright © LJ Ross, 2024
Extract from Poison Garden © LJ Ross, 2024
Cover artwork and map by Andrew Davidson
Cover layout by Riverside Publishing Solutions Limited

The moral right of the author has been asserted

Penguin Random House values and supports copyright. Copyright fuels creativity, encourages diverse voices, promotes freedom of expression and supports a vibrant culture. Thank you for purchasing an authorised edition of this book and for respecting intellectual property laws by not reproducing, scanning or distributing any part of it by any means without permission. You are supporting authors and enabling Penguin Random House to continue to publish books for everyone. No part of this book may be used or reproduced in any manner for the purpose of training artificial intelligence technologies or systems. In accordance with Article 4(3) of the DSM Directive 2019/790, Penguin Random House expressly reserves this work from the text and data mining exception.

Typeset by Riverside Publishing Solutions Limited

Printed and bound in Great Britain by Clays Ltd, Elcograf S.p.A.

The authorised representative in the EEA is Penguin Random House Ireland,
Morrison Chambers, 32 Nassau Street, Dublin D02 YH68

A CIP catalogue record for this book is available from the British Library

ISBN: 978-1-804-96035-6

Penguin Random House is committed to a sustainable future
for our business, our readers and our planet. This book is made
from Forest Stewardship Council® certified paper.

*"Even in the darkest moments,
hope is what holds us together."*

—Dan Jurgens, *The Death of Superman*

CHAPTER 1

Saturday, 23rd March

Northumberland

Of all the ruined castles of Northumberland, Dunstanburgh reigned supreme.

In the seven centuries since its foundations were first laid, walls had crumbled and wood rotted away with the winds that swept in with the relentless tide of the North Sea, but the fortress remained; rugged and magnificent atop its craggy headland, an imposing reminder that it would endure, long after the people who trampled over its remains were dead and gone.

Roger Aitken thought of this, and of his own mortality, as he approached the thirteenth tee of the Dunstanburgh Castle Golf Course. The course was situated to the north of the castle complex, and ran parallel to the sea, affording a beautiful view of Gull Crag—a sheer, vertical rockface that had once been a natural defence for the castle's northern perimeter, but was now a protected heritage site for birds and other sea life.

He paused, resting lightly against the club he carried, and lifted his head to the salty breeze that rolled in from the sea, which glimmered in the morning sunshine.

"It's a pretty sight, isn't it?" He nodded to another club member, Pete, who caught him up after a successful putt on the twelfth.

"Aye, it never gets old," he said, smiling proudly at the towering edifice that rose up like a mythical Camelot. "Makes you wonder what medieval soldiers thought, when they first caught sight of those walls."

"Probably wet themselves," the other man said, and wheezed a hearty laugh. "That's if they made it halfway up those rocks, or the hill on the other side, without gettin' an arrow between the eyes first."

The two men chatted for a while longer, exchanging mild gossip about who would be the next Men's Team Captain after old Kev's retirement. Naturally, both denied any interest whatsoever in taking up the role themselves, before Roger declared it was time he was getting along, while thinking privately that it was also high time he started canvassing for votes back at the clubhouse.

"Watch the crosswind on the thirteenth," Pete advised. "It's unlucky for some!"

Roger narrowed his eyes against the glare of the sun, breathed in the crisp air, and took a shot that landed within a foot of the hole.

"Not for me," he winked. Laughing at Pete's good-natured expletive, he sauntered towards the green, swinging the putter lightly in one hand while he looked out across the bay immediately to his left. It was known locally as 'Death Rocks', or 'Boulder Bay', on account of its large basalt rocks, which were dangerously slippery and had been the cause of many an unfortunate mishap over the years.

As he neared the green, he positioned himself and wiggled his hips for good measure, preparing to tap the ball into the hole. Before he could, there came a piercing shriek from one of the gulls circling the skies overhead, loud enough to break his concentration.

"Stupid birds," he muttered, and looked up to find an unusual number of them circling a spot near the edge of the course, where the long grass met the rocky shoreline.

Thinking it was likely to be a dead fish or some other carrion, Roger turned his attention back to the ball sitting neatly on the grass in front of him.

But the sound of the gulls continued, their cacophony only seeming to grow louder.

Unable to focus, he abandoned his putter on the ground and stomped towards the edge of the course, intending to chuck something to clear the flock and send them flapping elsewhere. He held up a hand to shield his eyes and peered across the dinosaur egg-shaped rocks to a spot a hundred yards away, where at least twenty gulls formed a cluster of excited, greedy chatter. It was impossible to see what they feasted upon, but, given their number, he assumed it was something larger than the usual wayward crab.

He cupped his hands and gave a loud shout.

It startled the birds for a moment, sending a few of them flapping up into the sky with an indignant cry, only to settle again within a matter of seconds.

Seconds was all he needed to catch sight of something colourful—and distinctly human.

A jacket? Trousers?

His skin prickled, a slow feeling of dread that crept along his spine.

Then, the gulls shifted, and he saw something else; something that could not be mistaken.

A hand.

The remains of a face.

"Everythin' all right, Roger? You look as if you've seen a ghost!"

Pete's voice called to him across the green, and with slow, careful steps, Roger backed away from the edge of the course, swallowing hard against the bile that lodged in his throat.

"Whatsamatter, man?" his friend puffed, having jogged the short distance between them. "You're not havin' a stroke, are you?"

Roger shook his head. "No," he muttered. "No…it's—it's over there, on the rocks. I think there's a body."

Pete's face registered comical shock. "A *body*? Are you sure?"

Roger nodded, and passed a shaking hand over his face as he tried to dispel the image.

"Maybe someone just turned their ankle, or banged their head and can't get up again?"

Pete started to move towards the rocks, but Roger put a staying hand on his arm.

"I'm telling you, the bloke's long gone. We need to call the police, that's what we need to do."

While the two men hurried back towards the clubhouse, the castle looked on, a silent sentinel keeping the secrets of all who passed beneath its shadow.

CHAPTER 2

One hour later

Detective Chief Inspector Maxwell Finley-Ryan, known simply as 'Ryan' to all who mattered, gripped the steering wheel of his car and resisted a strong urge to drive into oncoming traffic—even if it *would* provide the means to escape his sergeant's enthusiastic crooning to what, he was reliably informed, was "a proper eighties banger."

Detective Sergeant Frank Phillips began to tap the dashboard with invisible drumsticks, and Ryan's lips twitched.

"Frank, for the love of God, pull yourself together—"

Phillips wriggled a pair of ludicrously bushy eyebrows. "Sing along if you know it!"

Ryan couldn't prevent the smile that spread across his face, and, feeling like a prize idiot, began to sing in harmony with his friend, the pair of them wailing about Josie being on a vacation far away with cheerful abandon as they rattled northbound along the A1.

By the time they reached the turn-off for Dunstanburgh Castle, they'd covered much of the forty miles between Northumbria Police Headquarters in Newcastle upon Tyne and their destination, which was the pretty village of Craster, situated a mile and a half south of the castle ruins. They'd also managed to cover much of Spandau Ballet's back catalogue and made an impressive start on Billy Ocean.

Exhausted by his own efforts, Phillips enjoyed the passing scenery and folded his hands over his paunch—which was considerably less padded than before, thanks to a fearsome post-Christmas workout regime Denise had concocted with the help of one of her workout friends, Melissa, who'd christened his twice-weekly torture sessions, 'Turkey Burn Time'.

Sadists, the pair of them.

"What's the story wi' this one, then?"

Ryan recovered his voice. "I had a call from one of the local officers," he croaked. "You might remember she was the first attending officer when we had that business in Bamburgh, last year?"

Phillips made a rumbling sound of agreement. "Aye, nice lass. Knows her onions, and wants to get ahead."

Ryan nodded, because he'd come to much the same assessment of DC Charlie Reed. "Well, she caught another one," he said. "This time, it's a body on the beach up at Boulder Bay—"

"Death Rocks, you mean?"

Ryan might have lived in the North East for almost twenty years but, at times, he still felt like a visitor. "Is that what it's called?"

"Depends who you speak to," Phillips conceded. "I used to go up to Craster as a lad, and I remember the locals always used to call that stretch 'Death Rocks' and tell us to mind ourselves if we were playin' round that way."

"Well, it seems somebody didn't heed that warning," Ryan said. "A man was found dead on the rocks earlier this morning."

"If he slipped, what does Reed need us for?"

Ryan headed up the most senior team of murder detectives in that part of the world, under the umbrella of 'Major Crimes' within the Criminal Investigation Department of the Northumbria Police Constabulary. It tended to be serious or suspicious cases that drew their attention, and a simple accident, whilst unfortunate, didn't fall into either of those categories.

"Reed said something felt off about it, and wants a second opinion," Ryan explained. "I guess we'll find out when we get there. Faulkner's already on site, and I've put Pinter on notice that he's to expect a visitor to the mortuary within the next couple of hours." He referred to the senior Crime Scene Investigator, and the police pathologist who would perform a post-mortem examination in due course. "Just a minute," he added, peering at the GPS map on his car screen, then at a passing sign welcoming them to the village of Craster. "It would've made more sense to drive around to Embleton village or directly to the golf club, which is closer to the scene than Craster. Why did you suggest this route?"

Phillips tried to look innocent, and failed miserably. "All right, I'll level with you, son. Craster's known for the best kippers in the world; I tell you, it's *famous* for them—"

Ryan lowered his speed as they entered the village and, sure enough, the sign for *L Robson & Sons – Home of the 'Craster Kippers'* came into view.

"Are you trying to tell me that you deliberately misdirected me, so you could get your laughing gear around a kipper roll?"

Phillips nodded. "Well, I was actually hopin' for a kipper scotch egg, but let's not split hairs," he said, waving that away. "It'd be a tragedy not to stop in and sample one, while we're here. You could think of it as an exercise in community outreach—"

"All right, all right," Ryan muttered. "Don't gild the lily."

Phillips grinned to himself. "There's a nice walk from here to the castle," he added. "You can get around to the golf course from there, so it'll be just as easy."

Ryan sent him a withering look, but felt his own stomach respond to the scent of smoked kipper as they drove through the narrow streets of the old fishing village towards the harbour. Like so many of the little towns and villages dotted along the north-eastern coastline, it was a picturesque spot, with rows of stone-built cottages and colourful boats moored by the harbour wall. The local children were in school, but after three-fifteen they'd spill out of the school gates and line up for small bags of hot chips from the van parked outside the pub, or pick up an ice-cream to munch while looking out to sea.

It was a world away from the childhood he'd had; first, at the grand old house in Devon which had been in the Ryan family for generations, and then at boarding school while his father travelled the world as a diplomat. He didn't blame his parents for their decision to send him away, but, *ah*…how he'd have liked to walk home from school with an ice cream in his hand, and find his parents waiting for him with open arms.

"You alreet, lad?" Phillips had a keen eye.

"Yes," Ryan murmured, and brought the car to a stop. "I was thinking about Emma."

His daughter was now a precocious toddler, full of love and energy, and he wanted to keep her that way for as long as possible.

"Little darlin'," Phillips said warmly. "O' course, she's got her mother's looks, intelligence, charm and personality, so she'll go far."

Ryan laughed. "I can't argue with that," he said, and his eyes softened as he thought of his wife, Anna, who had given him the world. "Come on, let's fortify ourselves and hope we don't regret it when we see what's waiting for us on the other side of the castle."

Phillips, who wasn't known for having a particularly strong stomach, became serious as he weighed up the risks. "It's still worth it," he declared. "I'll take my chances."

Having shrugged into his all-weather jacket, Ryan made a grab for a couple of plastic bags, which he stuffed into one of the pockets. "I'm not taking any," he muttered.

CHAPTER 3

The walk from Craster towards the ruined castle of Dunstanburgh was a scenic stroll over gentle terrain, just as Phillips had promised. To their right, the North Sea lapped against the shoreline, a little choppy in the breeze, and, to their left, there was the remains of a medieval lake complex, built to sustain and to defend the castle which loomed large a mile or so further along the path. The castle was visible throughout their walk along the headland, at first appearing small against the horizon, but growing larger and more impressive with every step.

"Deceptive, isn't it?" Phillips declared. "From back there, it didn't seem like much, but as you get closer it's narf somethin', isn't it?"

Ryan nodded, and cast his eye over the gatehouse, then the mighty Lilburn Tower, which looked out all the way across to the equally impressive fortress at Bamburgh, further along the coast. It was a fearsome, awe-inspiring feat of architecture, and he could only imagine how it would have looked in all of its original glory.

"What's the story behind it?" he asked. "Anna's probably told me before, but…" He trailed off, guiltily.

"We can't all be history buffs," Phillips chuckled. "Don't worry, Uncle Frank'll give you a quick recap." He clasped the lapels of his overcoat, adopting what he considered to be a 'learned' stance, and promptly stepped into a steaming cow pat.

"Y' bugger!"

Ryan slapped a palm to his face, and laughed, while his sergeant hopped from one booted foot to the other, trying his best to dislodge the worst of it on a nearby tuft of grass.

"That's country living for you," Ryan remarked.

Phillips muttered something unintelligible, and gave a nearby cow the beady eye. "It's a bleedin' minefield out here," he complained.

After he'd cleaned himself off as best he could, they continued onward.

"Well, as you know, the castle sits between Craster and the village of Embleton, which is a bit further north of the golf course. It was built by the Earl of Lancaster in the fourteenth century," Phillips began.

"I'm not going to ask how you know all this," Ryan muttered.

"Common knowledge," Phillips said, loftily. "Now, this Lancaster was the leader of a rebel faction against the king at the time, who was Edward the…second or third?"

"Don't look at me," Ryan laughed, and held his hands up.

"The second," Phillips decided. "Anyhow, he built Dunstanburgh as a northern stronghold, in case things went downhill with the king, and as a flashy display of how wealthy he was. It doesn't hurt that it's just down the coast from the king's castle at Bamburgh, so that would have given people food for thought."

"Because it's just as big, you mean?"

"Maybe bigger," Phillips said. "Turns out, size does matter."

"Denise was saying the same thing to me, just the other day."

Phillips let out a bawdy laugh, and clapped his friend on the back. "Mind your cheek," he said, good-naturedly. "I tell you, she'll be the death of me, lad—"

Ryan could have kicked himself for having opened Pandora's Box. "*I'll* be the death of you, if you bang on again about your stamina after all these weekly workouts," Ryan said. "It's enough to give me nightmares."

Phillips laughed again. "All I'm sayin' is, when you get to my time of life, every little bit helps," he winked. "Now, where was I? Oh, aye. Lancaster built a big castle to show off about how rich and influential he was, so the king would know he was a force to be reckoned with. Unfortunately for him, he only got to visit his new castle once, before he was captured at the Battle of Boroughbridge. He was executed and the castle was given over to the Crown, anyhow."

Ryan raised a single black eyebrow. "So the moral of the story is, don't crow too loud, or the king'll chop your head off and snatch your castle?"

"Aye, pretty much," Phillips said. "The castle was reinforced over the centuries and put to use during the Wars of the Roses, but it was all rack and ruin after then. Once the Scottish border raids mostly stopped after James I came in, there wasn't much need of it as a military stronghold, so he sold it to the Grey family as a private residence. It's looked after by National Heritage now."

"It's a natural defensive spot, isn't it?" Ryan remarked, and paused at the foot of the hill leading up to the castle entrance to survey the landscape. You've got an enormous gatekeep on this side, and the sea to the east, with a natural harbour which can easily be defended. To the west, they made three lakes at the bottom of the crag, which would make access difficult, even without having to scale the hillside to reach the castle. Then, on the northern side, you've got Gull Crag. It's protected on all sides."

Phillips nodded, and then lowered his voice a fraction. "They say it's haunted—"

Ryan rolled his eyes. "Don't start that again."

"There were all sorts of strange goings-on, that Christmas we were over at Chillingham Castle," he argued. "You can't deny *that*."

"Imagination is a powerful thing," Ryan said.

"And don't forget the Pink Lady of Bamburgh," Phillips added.

"Who only comes out for tourists during peak season," Ryan drawled. "Very convincing, I'm sure."

"You're nowt but a cynic," Phillips decided. "It'll not be that, when Sir Guy the Seeker comes chasin' after you."

Ryan huffed out a sigh, and gave in to curiosity. "Come on, then. Who's Sir Guy the Seeker, when he's at home?"

"*Well*," Phillips said, in hushed tones. "He was a knight who arrived at the castle one stormy night, in desperate need of shelter. He was met by a wizard—"

"Who else?" Ryan wondered aloud.

"Shurrup, while I finish the story," Phillips chuckled. "Now, this wizard led him inside, where Sir Guy came across a beautiful lady inside a crystal tomb, guarded by a load of sleeping knights."

"They're always sleeping 'beauties'," Ryan said, sagely.

"It helps," Phillips agreed. "Anyway, Sir Guy had clocked her, and thought he wouldn't mind askin' her to the nearest banquet—"

Ryan grinned.

"He asked the wizard how to set her free, and the wizard told him to choose between a sword or a hunting horn—Sir Guy chose the horn. It woke up the sleeping knights, the wizard told him he was a prize chump, and Sir Guy woke up in the gate-porch, soakin' wet from the rain, with no horse and the castle door barred to him. Legend says he was so determined to get back inside and choose again, he didn't eat, drink or sleep, so he died of exposure."

Phillips paused, for dramatic effect.

"Now, his ghost roams the castle searching for the door to the lady's tomb, but never finding it, or her…"

Ryan held up a hand. "So let me see if I've got this right. Some poor, half-starved bloke arrived at the castle on an old nag one filthy night, hoping for a bed and a bowl of soup. Instead, he finds the doors locked, so he huddles inside the porch in the driving rain, and probably passes out and dreams or hallucinates seeing the woman of his dreams. Eventually, he wakes up, only to find himself sitting out in the cold, and promptly goes off his proverbial rocker. Correct?"

Phillips pursed his lips to hide a smile. "Well, I s'pose that's *one* way of puttin' it," he said. "But I like my version better."

Ryan nodded towards the castle keep. "Well, I think I can safely say it won't be Sir Guy the Seeker we find washed up on Death Rocks."

"Couldn't blame him for givin' up the search," Phillips said. "I don't remember the footpath being as long as this, back when I was a nipper."

"C'mon, Frank," Ryan said, slinging an arm around his sergeant's broad shoulders. "Where's your stamina when you need it?"

With a wicked laugh, he began to stride along the footpath that led around the castle to Death Rocks.

"The younger generation," Phillips grumbled, as he trotted behind. "No respect for their elders…oh *balls!*"

He'd stepped into another cow pat and, when he cast around for the culprit, he could have sworn it was the same one as before.

CHAPTER 4

"Have you heard from her?"

Detective Constable Jack Lowerson looked up to find his friend, and senior officer in the police hierarchy, watching him with kind, green eyes. "Not for a few weeks," he admitted, and felt his chest tighten. "The last I heard, Mel was going to be travelling around Thailand and Cambodia, so she's probably been too busy."

Detective Inspector Denise MacKenzie sat back in her chair and swivelled from side to side as she considered what would be the best response to give the young man who was, it was plain to see, thoroughly heartbroken. Jack had never been lucky in love—or perhaps it was more accurate to say he'd never been a terribly good judge of character—but it seemed his fortunes had changed when he met their colleague, Melanie Yates. The pair had been happy for a while, and lived together—with a cat—but neither could have predicted the turn of events that Fate had in store. First, that the murderer of Melanie's twin sister would be discovered, after more than fifteen years without a trace, and then, that Melanie herself would fall victim to the same hands. It was a miracle she'd survived, and testament to her own tenacity and grit, but she was only human and the trauma of such an ordeal took an inevitable toll. She'd taken an extended leave of absence from the constabulary, and, it seemed, from her life with Jack.

To heal, she'd said.

MacKenzie had suffered a similar nightmare herself, years before, and was therefore uniquely placed to understand the impact of post-traumatic stress on work and relationships. She couldn't blame Melanie for seeking a change of scene, but had to wonder whether that was truly the case—or if she was running away from real life, which could never truly be outrun.

"That's probably it," she said, quietly. "Remember what Melanie said, before she left;

she wanted the space to find herself again, which is something she probably can't do if she's in contact all the time."

Jack nodded, miserably. "Part of me understands," he said. "But another part of me just feels...*angry*." He scrubbed his hands over his face, which was gaunt and unshaven. "I don't have any right to feel that way," he added. "I'm not the one who had to go through that ordeal—"

"No, but you supported her through everything," MacKenzie put in. "You're allowed to feel abandoned, Jack. Nobody blames you for that, and we're here whenever you need to talk."

He looked across at the woman who had, in many ways, been like an older sister to him. "Thanks, Mac," he said. "I appreciate it, and all the dinners and Sunday lunches. It's meant a lot."

She smiled. "You're like family to us," she said. "Besides, you never have to thank me for letting you come around and entertain Samantha for a few hours."

He laughed, thinking of the countless games of Monopoly and Scrabble he'd endured at the merciless hands of their adopted daughter. "She takes no prisoners," he said, with admiration.

"You can say that again," MacKenzie chuckled. "Did I tell you, she won first prize at the show-jumping the other day?"

Jack smiled, remembering that Samantha's greatest and only friend when she'd come to Frank and Denise had been her horse, Pegasus. She might not have had a traditional education in her formative years, but she was a gifted horsewoman and had a natural affinity with animals of all description.

"That's fantastic," he said. "I can just see Frank hob-knobbing with all those horsey types."

"So long as he doesn't get any ideas about jumping on the back of one himself, I don't mind who he hob-knobs with," she said. "The last thing I need is Frank laid up with a broken ankle, ringing a bell for bacon sandwiches and cups of tea every five minutes."

They both grinned, then Jack became serious once more. "Do you think she'll ever come back?" he asked, softly.

MacKenzie reached across the expanse of desk and gave his hand a quick squeeze. "I honestly don't know, but one thing I do know is that you'll be absolutely fine either way. Remember that, Jack. You're a good man, and deserve to be happy."

His eyes strayed to a framed picture of himself with Melanie in better days, smiling in the sunshine on a day out at the beach.

He looked away, sharply.

"Better crack on," he said, with forced cheer. "These criminals won't catch themselves, eh?"

"Fancy a cuppa before we hunt them down?"

"Go on, then."

Detective Constable Charlie Reed was feeling the effects of a fourth consecutive night without sleep, thanks to the wakeful exuberance of her two-year-old son, who'd apparently taken the unilateral decision that sleep was for the weak. She'd given up trying to convince him otherwise sometime around four in the morning, and had entertained him with a *Peppa Pig* marathon, which he'd watched while munching his way through a bowl of porridge. Consequently, Charlie had been awake for several hours by the time the call came through reporting a body up at Death Rocks. With Ben safely with his grandma by that time, she'd risked a caffeine-induced heart attack by downing her fifth coffee of the morning, and made her way up to the golf club at Dunstanburgh to perform her duties, alongside a young PC by the name of Dave Waddell, who was not, it was fair to say, the sharpest tool in the box.

"Have you forgotten something?" she asked him, for the umpteenth time.

The young man stared at her vacantly.

"You're supposed to be standing guard at the scene, logging anyone who comes or goes," she said, barely keeping the frustration from her voice. "I'm here at the clubhouse taking down statements, but I need you out there"—she jabbed a finger towards the course, which was visible through a wall of windows in the function room—"to protect the site. It's basic training, Waddell."

"I needed a slash, Guv," he admitted.

His response induced no sympathy from her whatsoever. "This isn't primary school," she snapped. "You've had the whole morning to drain your radiator, and it isn't time for a break, as you're fully aware. Bugger off to the gents so you don't make a puddle on the floor—but if you think you'll have time to scroll for sports fixtures on your phone, you've got another thing coming, because if you're in there for longer than *five minutes*, I'll come and drag you out myself. Is that clear?"

He nodded vigorously and she made a show of checking her watch.

"*Go!*"

Waddell scurried off, and hoped the fear of reprisals wouldn't induce 'stage fright' at the crucial moment. In the wake of his departure, there came a brief round of applause, and she turned to find Ryan and Phillips standing a few feet behind her, in the foyer of the clubhouse.

"I was about to ask which muppet was responsible for leaving the scene wide open, but you've already got things well in hand," Ryan said, approvingly. "Nice to see you again, Reed."

He held out a hand, which she shook.

"You too, sir—and Sergeant Phillips. It's been a few months, hasn't it?"

"Frank," he said, easily. "Aye, not been too many grisly murders up in this neck o' the woods for a while. Maybe they're all off on holiday, murderin' in the Balearics instead."

"Well, the sun's out again, so maybe this one marks the beginning of a new season," she said, with a certain dark humour they both appreciated.

"Tell us about the body on the beach," Ryan said, and tucked his hands into his pockets. "I take it something feels suspicious or you wouldn't have asked us up here."

She nodded. "I'm probably being over-zealous—"

"No such thing, in this business," Ryan assured her. "Instinct is vastly underrated by the Powers That Be, but, in my experience, it's one of the best tools we have."

"Put another way," Phillips chimed in, "if you smell a rabbit off, then it's probably off."

They looked at him in confusion. "Who said anything about *rabbits*?" Ryan burst out.

"You know what I mean," Phillips said. "You can always tell when somethin' or someone isn't the full shillin'."

Ryan rolled his eyes. "Now you're talking about coinage that hasn't been in circulation for fifty years?"

"Well, what do you namby-pamby southerners say, then?" Phillips cried. *"Things aren't altogether as they seem, therefore I shall be approaching the situation with caution?"*

There was a pause, and then Ryan shrugged. "Well…yes, actually."

Now, it was Phillips who rolled his eyes. "No wonder you don't believe in ghosts," he muttered.

Sensing it was an opportune moment, Reed cut in. "Well, I can tell you that I definitely smelled a rabbit off, and that things weren't quite the full shilling," she said, deadpan. "I felt it was best to approach the situation with caution."

Both men smiled at her.

"I like this un," Phillips said to his friend, in a stage whisper.

"Let's take it from the top," Ryan said. "When did the call come through?"

"Control Room took a call from a local man, Roger Aitken, shortly after nine-thirty this morning," she replied, all business now. "He'd been out for an early round of golf with another member of the club, Peter Jenkins. I've taken preliminary statements from both witnesses, but they're in the lounge area if you'd like to speak with either of them. Apparently, Roger spotted the body over on the rocks as he was putting on the thirteenth hole, which is at the far end, closest to the castle, sir."

"No need for 'sir'," Ryan said, as an aside.

She nodded her thanks, and felt some of the tension in her shoulders begin to drain away. Her last experience working with Ryan had been faultless, but he carried a reputation for demanding the best from his staff and she was conscious that maternal exhaustion wasn't always conducive to positive outcomes at work. She couldn't give one hundred per cent to every element of her life, and some days she felt she was stretched very thin.

"I was dispatched alongside PC Waddell, who's a recent transfer from Berwick—"

"I *knew* I recognised that lad from somewhere!" Phillips exclaimed. "He was one of the bobbies at the scene up in Lady's Well, remember?"

Recognition gleamed in Ryan's eyes. "The wally with the chocolate eyeballs," he muttered, darkly. "I remember." He turned to his sergeant. "Don't even *think* about asking him whether he's carrying any with him, this time," he said, and pointed a finger at Phillips' chest. "You've only just burned off the turkey, remember?"

"I never even *thought* of it," the other man lied.

Unconvinced, Ryan turned back to Reed, who looked between them with unconcealed delight.

"Don't ask," he advised her. "Carry on."

"Thank you," she said, gravely. "As I was saying, we got here at about quarter to ten. Paramedic staff were already on site and had declared the male 'deceased', following which I made a brief assessment of the scene and instructed Waddell to begin securing the site from public interference. I enlisted a couple of other PCs to close access via the Craster pathway, which I hope was correct."

"Absolutely," Ryan said. "We saw the police line. I imagine National Heritage aren't going to be happy about the closure, since it restricts access to the castle."

"One of their representatives has already been in touch," she said. "As you say, they weren't best pleased. However, I explained the situation, and they were very understanding; they've said they'll do all they can to cooperate."

Ryan smiled, and thought that, if her diplomacy skills were anything to go by, DC Reed could prove herself to be a useful person to have around.

"I also explained the need for *confidentiality*," she added. "But it's a small community, so I imagine word will spread very quickly."

"Yes." Ryan nodded. "It's also a popular tourist spot, and the weather is tipped for glorious sunshine, at least for the next couple of days—"

Phillips snorted. "Any time somebody tells me we're in for a bit of sunshine, first thing I pick up's an umbrella."

"Couldn't agree more," Ryan said. "But the tourists don't know the weather forecasts around here are about as reliable as a chocolate fireguard, so they'll still be arriving in their droves. The important thing is to keep the pathways clear so that Faulkner's team have the best chance of recovering evidence from the wider castle site, if they need to."

Charlie nodded. "Faulkner's looking over the body now," she said, and, through the windows, they could see the outline of a forensics tent billowing on the breeze. "We've already made an identification."

"Oh? Who is it?" Phillips asked.

"William Harding," she replied. "He's a photographer. Faulkner found some ID on his person, but I'd already run the plates on one of the cars sitting in the car park, which the Club Secretary seemed to think had been left overnight. It belongs to Mr Harding. I haven't been able to locate a 'next of kin' yet, and I wanted to speak to you first, regarding whether to designate the case 'suspicious' or not, before speaking to the family."

"Good idea," Ryan said. "We can afford another hour, especially as it seems likely Harding was lying out on the rocks throughout the night. I presume he parked up in the evening and walked down to the beach to take pictures, then lost his footing and sustained a serious head injury. Without help, it's possible he could have died slowly during the night."

"It certainly has some of the hallmarks of an accidental death," Reed said. "Harding was actually hired to come and take pictures of a retirement party held here at the clubhouse last night. The placement of the body would suggest that, at some point, he went outside to take pictures of the castle beneath the stars, had an accident on the rocks and never came back to the party. His absence wasn't noticed, because the place was heaving with members enjoying themselves until well past midnight."

"But?" Ryan prompted her. "I feel a 'but' coming on."

Charlie inclined her head. "*But* it was also very overcast, last night. It doesn't make any sense to me that a photographer would head out into the cold, hike down to the thirteenth hole and across the rocks to that particular spot to take a picture of a shadowy outline of the castle in almost complete darkness."

Phillips made a sound of appreciation. "Now, *that's* what I call having a nose for the business," he said. "As the lass rightly says, why would anyone, let alone a professional, go to all that trouble just to take a picture of nowt? On a good night, you'd be able to see the castle's outline against the Milky Way, or silhouetted by the moon, but not when the clouds are coverin' everythin' up."

Ryan nodded slowly. "Was a camera found beside him?" he asked.

"Yes, but it's broken, and missing a memory card," Reed replied. "Faulkner's bagged it up for testing."

Ryan looked around the room, and his eye fell upon a man somewhere in his late fifties, who was seated beside one of the far windows staring out to sea.

"Is that the Club Secretary?" he asked.

Reed nodded. "John Dawson," she provided. "I was about to take a formal statement from him."

"You do that," he said. "Frank? Let's go and have a word with Faulkner."

Phillips' stomach gave an audible rumble of warning. "Ah, you know, I thought I should stay here and…lend a hand."

Ryan raised an eyebrow, and Phillips laid it on a bit thicker, just to be sure.

"Besides," he said, in a fragile tone. "What with these hips of mine, it's not safe for an old codger like me to go scampering over the rocks—"

"Frank, I watched you put a man down in the boxing ring at Buddles just the other day," Ryan protested. "I've seen you dance on tables and stages around the North East like you were John Travolta. Don't give me any of that blarney."

Phillips cast a meaningful glance down at Ryan's feet. "Think of those nice, clean boots," he purred.

Ryan narrowed his eyes. "You wouldn't."

Phillips patted his belly. "Better safe than sorry…"

Ryan turned to DC Reed, who struggled to contain her laughter. "Just say 'no' if he suggests taking a stottie break," he hissed, and then stalked off towards the door leading out onto the course.

CHAPTER 5

Death was never pretty, and this was never more so than in the case of Will Harding.

His body lay against the rocks, a crumple of skin and bone laid bare to the elements, cased inside the torn and sodden remains of an expensive black suit. His face was an ashen grey mask, no longer possessed of eyes or features, thanks to the birds who'd taken sustenance from his shell. To many, it was a horrifying sight; something to haunt their nightmares and intrude upon their waking hours and remind them of their own mortality. But for Tom Faulkner, death was so much a part of life that he no longer viewed it as something to be feared—rather as something to be studied with a clinical eye for detail.

He looked up from an inspection of Harding's hands to see a tall, raven-haired man enter the forensics tent.

"Morning, Tom!" Ryan dipped beneath the tarpaulin into the stifling interior, which carried the ripe scent of death despite a fresh wind rushing under the tent walls.

"Morning," Faulkner replied, and stood up for a moment to stretch out the kinks in his back. "No Phillips today?"

"He's up at the clubhouse, preserving his stomach."

Tom laughed, and shook his head. "Considering the state of the body, that's probably a wise decision," he said. "This poor guy's been out here for hours…I'll leave it to the pathologist to give a more precise estimate but, from experience, I'd guess at least ten."

Ryan crouched down and, with a gloved hand, gently tested the movement of one of the man's arms, which he found stiff and cold.

"I'd agree with that, which would take our estimated time of death to somewhere around midnight, or possibly earlier," he said, and straightened up again, frowning slightly at the condition of the skin on Harding's face. "Did you turn him over?"

Faulkner shook his head. "You never miss a trick," he said. "I guess you're thinking of the mottling on his skin? I noticed it too. As you know, that usually happens when the blood stops circulating and succumbs to gravity, settling on the lowest point of the body. That would suggest our man here was lying face-down, immediately post mortem."

Ryan looked around the rocks at their feet, stuck his head outside the tent for a moment, then scrutinized the body once more.

"The rocks directly beneath us here are above the tide line," he said. "It's therefore unlikely the water played any part in rolling him around, especially not a full one-hundred-and-eighty degrees."

Faulkner nodded. "Reed said the same thing," he replied. "I suggested to her that it's possible he was dislodged or chivvied about by the wildlife; the gulls around here are enormous, and, with enough clout behind them, it's very possible they could have rolled him over."

Ryan nodded slowly. "Surely there'd have been abrasion marks?"

"Again, that's a matter for Pinter to investigate," Faulkner replied. "But bear in mind, you wouldn't see ordinary bruising if he was already dead and, in any case, it's very difficult to distinguish one type of abrasion mark from another now that the birds have been at him."

Ryan looked upon the sorry remains of a man and, steeling himself against the horror, crouched down again to inspect the contusion marks around the dead man's face and skull.

"There seem to be two major injuries," he said, after a minute. "Here, on the forehead, and a larger fracture to the back of his head."

Faulkner agreed. "Yes, although, as I say—"

"The birds haven't helped, I know," Ryan murmured. "Still, the injury to the back of the skull looks significant; more than the peck of a bird's beak. Have you found any blood or brain matter on any of the surrounding rocks?"

Faulkner shook his head. "Nope, not a thing so far. We haven't finished yet, mind you. We've got a few hours ahead of us to comb the surrounding area, and it'll go into the next day or so if you want us to fan out as far as the castle."

Ryan rocked back on his heels, considered prosaic matters such as resources and budgets, then stood up again. "Do it," he said. "I happen to agree with DC Reed on this one, Tom. We've got a man whose positioning doesn't match the likely trajectory of his fall, and, so far, no obvious sign of the impact site. His camera is found without a memory card, which makes no sense if he was in the area specifically to take pictures."

"Could've popped out when he fell," Faulkner suggested. "The impact broke the camera, so the card might have flown wide of the body."

"If you find it, I'll update my assessment," Ryan said. "Until then, I'm treating this one as suspicious. Anything else you can tell me, before I start shaking down the locals?"

Faulkner shook his head. "No obvious defensive marks, no torn fingernails," he said. "We found a few fibres here and there, so I'll get them off for testing as soon as I can."

"Thanks Tom."

Ryan made as if to leave, then turned back, as if remembering himself. "By the way, some of us are getting together for a couple of jars on

Friday…nothing fancy, just a few beers and a few laughs, if you'd like to join us?"

Faulkner smiled. "Love to—what's the occasion?"

Ryan was awkward, all of a sudden. "Apparently, I'm turning forty. Age is catching up with me."

Faulkner nodded towards the unfortunate soul at their feet. "Better than the alternative," he quipped. "I'll be there to toast your milestone, Grandpa."

Ryan flashed a grin, and was gone.

CHAPTER 6

The Club Secretary was a short, pot-bellied man by the name of John Dawson and, within the first five minutes of their acquaintance, Phillips and Reed were both firmly of the opinion that, when given into the wrong hands, trivial, bureaucratic powers could create an officious monster of even the most mild-tempered individual. Phillips would later remark that he'd seen it happen predominantly in cases of driving test examiners, traffic wardens, and, he was sorry to say, those in charge of freshly-baked goods at his local supermarket. Keeping in mind Ryan's warning on the subject of stottie cakes, Reed chose not to enquire further.

"Thank you for all your help this morning, Mr Dawson," she did say, when the three were seated at one of the tables in the clubhouse bar.

Dawson nodded, and twiddled his thumbs in a manner that managed to be both distracting and irritating in equal measure. "Well, you know, club matters are *my* responsibility, and ensuring members can access the facilities at all times is a key priority."

"Very laudable," Phillips said. "For now, we're a bit less concerned about member services and a bit more concerned about the poor bloke lying out on the rocks."

Dawson was instantly contrite. "Well, naturally...of course, I didn't mean to suggest that the club was more important than your investigation, sergeant. I was very shocked when I heard what had happened to William."

"Who told you?" Reed asked, without looking up from her notepad.

"Oh, Roger mentioned it," Dawson replied. "I was pottering around here when I saw the pair of them—him and Pete, that is—legging it back across the grass. It would have been faster for them if they'd taken one of the carts out, but they like a good stretch of the legs."

"So they told you about the body," Reed confirmed, as she made scribbled notes in a small pad.

Dawson nodded. "Yes, they said they needed to call the police, so I let them use the phone in the office," he said. "Their mobile phones were both locked away in their lockers, so it seemed faster."

Reed nodded. "And what time did you arrive here at the clubhouse, this morning?"

"I was here from eight-thirty," he said. "I opened the doors, in case anyone fancied an early round to shake off the cobwebs, and I also wanted to make sure the cleaners had made a start with the clean-up operation, after last night's party."

Phillips eyed some half-inflated balloons in the corner, and, with his fine nose for sugar, could scent cake on the air, which told him leftovers were not far away.

As if she'd read his mind, Reed moved on to her next question. "We understand Mr Harding was engaged to come and take some pictures at the party last night—can you tell us who hired him?"

"That was me," Dawson said. "I'd seen his work on Instagram, and heard good things in general. He did landscapes, mostly, but also the occasional wedding and special event, so I got in touch to ask if he was free to come along. He gave me a good price, so I booked him in. Kev—Kevin Kincade, that is—was our Men's Team Captain for a number of years, so he deserved to go out with a bang."

"What time was Harding due to arrive and finish?"

"The agreement was for him to come at six-thirty, for a seven o'clock start. It gave him time to grab a sandwich and take a look around the clubhouse to get his bearings."

"Harding hadn't been here before?"

"No, he said it was his first time, although he's photographed the castle many times over the years," Dawson replied. "He's not local to the area; I understand he lived somewhere in town."

By 'town' they presumed he meant Newcastle, but they'd check the details later.

"The idea was for him to blend into the crowd and capture all the special moments, the speeches at dinner and all that, *reportage* style," Dawson continued. "He had a few breaks throughout the night, but otherwise he just moved around the crowd snapping pictures. He was due to finish at eleven-thirty."

"Do you remember the last time you saw him?" Reed asked.

Dawson puffed out his cheeks. "Must've been sometime around ten-thirty," he said. "I remember seeing him chatting to one of the waitresses at the bar, and—" He broke off, not wishing to speak ill of the dead.

"Go on," Reed urged him. "It's important you give us a full account."

"Well, I was only going to say that he was spending a fair amount of time *flirting*, when he should have been *working*," Dawson said, and pursed his lips tightly, like the arse-end of a cat. "Come to think of it, I didn't see him at all after then."

"And the girl?" Reed asked.

"Molly," Dawson provided. "She was serving behind the bar until midnight."

They made a note of her name and home address, and the same details of the other staff who'd worked at the party the previous evening.

"Do you have a full list of all the members present here, last night?" Phillips asked him.

"Yes," Dawson said, and looked between the pair of them. "But…I'm sorry, I'm a bit confused. I thought Harding fell and was killed accidentally. If that's the case, why would you need to speak with all the attendees?"

"We haven't yet determined whether Mr Harding died accidentally or otherwise," Reed replied. "We'll need to take statements from everyone."

"My goodness," Dawson breathed, and ran a hand over his remaining hair. "I suppose, I assumed—"

"Because of the rocks?" Phillips put in. "Aye, seems very neat, doesn't it?"

Dawson nodded. "I don't think Harding could have known anyone at the party last night, unless he happens to have family or friends living in this area," he said. "None of our staff had met him before, nor had I. Frankly, I can't understand what other possible explanation there could be for his death, besides an accident."

In point of fact, neither could they.

"That's for us to investigate," Phillips said, cheerfully. "Nothing like a good mystery, you know."

Dawson said nothing for a moment, no doubt worrying about how long his member services would be disrupted.

"If there's anything else I can do to help, just ask."

Reed snapped her notepad shut and looked across to Phillips, who gave a small shake of his head.

"Just that list of attendees would be great, Mr Dawson—and access to any CCTV footage you may have, please."

He looked apologetic. "I'm sorry to say, we don't have much in the way of a camera system. I've been lobbying the members for funds to update it, for their own security, but so far without much joy. At the moment, there's coverage of the main doors, the bar area and the car park, but that's about it."

"It's a start," Phillips declared. "If you'll point us in the right direction, we'll have a gander at it."

Dawson nodded, and started to rise.

"One other thing," Reed said, quietly. "If you could ask those members who've started coming in to please vacate the clubhouse, we'd appreciate it."

He slumped back into his chair.

"The *clubhouse*? But—Harding died on the beach. Why do we need to disrupt the members here?"

Reed did not reply directly. "We like to turn over every stone, Mr Dawson."

CHAPTER 7

While the team at Dunstanburgh went about the business of turning over every stone they could find—both literal and metaphorical—MacKenzie stepped in for Ryan to chair a briefing at Northumbria CID Headquarters. The numbers were scant, not only because half of their small team was already absent, but because the case itself was fast becoming cold and the usual number of intelligence analysts and other support staff had been redeployed to work on more active investigations. Consequently, Denise found herself looking at precisely one other face across the conference table.

"Well," she said, and spread her hands to encompass the empty chairs. "Seems a bit pointless taking up a meeting room, when it's just the two of us. D' you fancy going for a wander down to the river, and we can talk over the case while we're at it?"

Jack perked up considerably at the prospect, and scraped back his chair with indecent haste.

"Whatever the boss says! Do you need me to bring a summary note?"

"No, I remember the facts of the case, and—spoiler alert—there haven't been any developments," she replied, and held open the door for him to precede her. "The idea of the briefing is to refresh our memories to see if we can come up with any bright ideas about a fresh angle to take, which we can do just as well on the go."

"Sunshine and a takeaway coffee never hurt anyone," he agreed. "Maybe a walk will help loosen up our institutionalised brain cells."

"You can say that again," she muttered. "It's been a long winter of grim domestic cases and senseless violence."

"The stats for suicide and accidental death have really spiked this winter, as well," he remarked, as they made a beeline for the ground floor of the building, and the freedom that awaited them beyond. "I know that winter is always a bad season for it, but there seem to have been especially high numbers recently, don't you think?"

MacKenzie considered the question. "Come to think of it, you're right," she said.

They crossed the main foyer, waved a cheerful 'goodbye' to the desk sergeant as they went, and stepped outside onto the forecourt of the car park. By mutual accord, they stood there for a moment, letting the rays of the sun bathe their pasty faces while they sucked fresh air into their lungs.

"It's only when you come outside, you realise how much that place stinks of sweat," she grumbled, and then began walking towards the Pie Van, which was parked just outside the security entrance and promised fresh coffees in craft paper cups. "I wouldn't read too much into the statistics, Jack. If you looked at the curve of crime rates over a long period of time, you'd see that, as a whole, violent crime has vastly reduced in the past hundred years or more. If that's the case, why do we have people consistently complaining that crime is on the rise, and that they feel unsafe in their own homes?"

It was a rhetorical question, but she let him answer it.

"Perception," he replied. "The tabloids need click-bait, and nothing gets people clicking faster than a gruesome, human-interest story like murder. They sensationalise it, recycle the same story again and again, and end up giving people the impression violent crime is rife."

"Exactly," she said, and stepped up to the window to place an order for a couple of strong coffees, throwing in a couple of hand-baked doughnuts at the last minute. "I'm trying to support Frank in his fitness journey, so I've been avoiding having too many sweet treats around the house," she explained. "It's been torture."

Jack laughed, and took a healthy bite. "Thanks," he said, and took a swig of coffee to wash it down. "Your secret's safe with me—I'm your accomplice in illicit sugar consumption, now."

"Back to crime rates," she said, after savouring her first bite. "If you consider more specific demographics, then the statistics start to look a bit different."

"Gender's another good example of that," he said. "We all know, statistically, that by far the biggest demographic to die by murder is male. Then again, they're also the biggest group of perpetrators—"

"Male on male violence is the most lethal, statistically," she agreed.

"Right. But it becomes a bit more nuanced when you look at the circumstances," he said. "Those male deaths tend to come out of random violent attacks outside pubs and clubs, gang-related violence or that sort of thing, whereas, when women are killed, in the vast majority of cases it's by someone they know, intimately."

They walked quietly for a while, enjoying the sun on their backs and the food in their bellies, until they came to the riverside. They stood watching the water, then MacKenzie spoke up again, this time about a male victim who had died in none of the circumstances they'd spoken of, but by other means entirely.

"Let's talk about Marcus Atherton," she said. "He's the reporter from the *Daily Chronicle* who was found dead in his own home. It's been four months and we've found nothing suspicious to justify keeping this case open, but Ryan is adamant that we keep looking. What do you make of it?"

Jack rested his forearms on the railing, watched a sea bird swoop down to nab a fish, and thought of his friend and mentor. Ryan might have seemed like a maverick to the untrained eye—or indeed, to their Chief Constable—but he was meticulous in his work, logical in his approach to investigation, and able to detach himself completely from the emotive elements of a case, even under extreme pressure. For him, instinct was a tool, but not one that was ever trusted above proven facts, and he was not in the habit of wasting police time. Therefore, if he felt there was something to find, he must truly believe it was there to be found.

"Remind me of the details, will you?"

MacKenzie leaned back against the railing, and crossed her feet at the ankles. "There isn't much to tell," she said. "Atherton lived alone and was found dead on the floor of his living room by the window cleaners, of all people, who happened to look in as they were doing their regular monthly clean. No defensive wounds or marks found on the body. Autopsy revealed the cause of death to be carbon monoxide poisoning and, when the gas fire in his living room was checked, it was found to be faulty—so that all adds up, so far."

He nodded, picturing the scene.

"We sent his mobile phone off to Digital Forensics," she continued. "They managed to unlock it, but there were no threatening messages, nothing obvious at all to suggest an outside threat. However, there were no fingerprints found on the phone—"

Jack looked across at her. "None at all?"

She shook her head. "Not a single one, which is why Ryan is like a dog with a bone—he thinks somebody wiped the phone clean, and, to be honest, I can't think of any other explanation for why there wasn't a print or even the fragment of a print found on the device. In this day and age, considering how much people rely on their phones, you'd have thought it would be covered in partials from Atherton himself."

"Mm," Lowerson said. "And, if I remember rightly, Faulkner's team didn't pick up any other forensic leads from the scene, either?"

"No, nothing," MacKenzie said. "Which, again, is unusual. You'd have thought there'd be a couple of unexplained DNA samples, because there always are, in every case. In this one, Atherton's home was sparkling clean."

"Which is suspicious," Jack said. "But what can we do, if we've already exhausted the usual forensics and questioned everyone at his office and in his personal life, and it's brought up precisely zilch?"

"I've already had his phone sent off to the Cyber Terrorism Unit in London," she said. "They can do a deeper dive and see if the phone's memory has a record of any deleted items that can be recovered. Unfortunately, a carbon monoxide death isn't exactly a priority, just as it wasn't a priority for the local digital forensics unit when we were first investigating. It's only going to be worse at a national level."

Lowerson agreed, and tried to think of another way. "We could contact the phone network and check Atherton's calls and messages against what's stored on the phone's memory, to see if anything's been deleted?"

MacKenzie nodded. "Same for his browsing history," she said. "We'll get in touch with the internet provider to see if anything was interfered with on his laptop."

"Ryan wanted to do this from the beginning, but Morrison put the brakes on," Jack said. "She might do the same again."

"We'll just have to make a case for the expenditure," MacKenzie said. "We're not giving up yet."

They both experienced a strange shiver, as if someone had walked upon their graves.

"That was weird," Jack said. "Did you feel that?"

"Yeah," she replied, and rubbed her arms to warm them. "Probably just getting a bit chilly out here. Let's start making our way back."

They retraced their steps, and couldn't escape the feeling that somebody, somewhere, had been listening.

CHAPTER 8

As the clock struck four, DC Reed began to feel a rising sense of anxiety, which had nothing to do with unexplained deaths, pernickety club secretaries or the unpleasant odour emanating from the gents toilets since PC Waddell had relieved himself. The fact was, she needed to leave soon in order to collect her son, but couldn't do so without first handing over management of the scene to one of her senior colleagues, neither of which were anywhere to be found—

"Reed?"

She turned, with palpable relief, to find Ryan striding through the doors of the clubhouse. "Sir—"

"I thought we'd dispensed with all that," he said, crisply. "Look, I'm going to have to call it a day. I promised I'd be home in time to read Emma's bedtime story, and I've got to head back to the office before then, so I need to shake a leg." He paused. "Which reminds me—you've got a little one as well, haven't you?"

She nodded. "He's at nursery, too," she said.

Ryan checked his watch, then read the stress on her face which she was trying very hard to hide. "Home time, then," he pronounced. "Thanks for a good job well done today."

She lifted her chin. "I can come in early tomorrow," she began, having been so used to making concessions that the words just fell out of her mouth.

He frowned, remembering that she was also a single parent. "*No*, you won't," he said. "I'll draft someone in to cover things, so you don't have to rush to get here at the crack of dawn. It's hard enough getting them fed and dressed, never mind actually leaving them without feeling all kinds of guilt, especially if you're managing everything solo. Do yourself a favour and get here when you get here."

She stared at him, at this tall, good-looking man who'd seen death of every description, and thought it surreal that they were speaking of the everyday juggle of parenting young children.

"I—thank you," she said.

"Who's your direct report?"

She folded her lips, loyalty ingrained in every line of her body. "I work with DI Finnegan," she said.

Ryan knew that Rod Finnegan was one of the old-fashioned relics in their Constabulary, and certainly not a man likely to consider the needs of a young working mother. "This is a personal question, so don't feel you have to answer," he said, but took the risk and asked it, all the same. "Do you have any help with—"

"Ben," she whispered.

"Ben," he repeated, and gave her an encouraging smile. "Only, I know it can be hard for my wife and me, at times, and there's two of us. Anna's parents are both dead, and mine live hundreds of miles away. A babysitter can be a godsend and, of course, friends can be very kind, but they have their own lives and families, don't they?"

She nodded, and swallowed hard against a sudden urge to tell him everything, and lean on someone for a change.

"My mam helps whenever she can," Charlie replied. "But she suffers from multiple sclerosis, which is progressing quite swiftly, and I'm going to have to move to be nearer to her in Newcastle because she lives alone; my dad was in the military, but he died a few years ago."

She said the last with as much detachment as she could muster.

"Won't that mean more of a commute to the Alnwick station here?" he enquired.

She nodded. "I'll make it work," she said. "I'm grateful to have my job, and I love my work, so we'll figure something out."

She had to.

Ryan nodded, understanding more and more. "Have you mentioned your circumstances to DI Finnegan?"

She gave another brief nod. "He said he would consider the situation," she replied. "But, obviously, the needs of the Constabulary come first."

She didn't bother to mention the numerous appeals she'd made to him for more flexible working hours, or even a transfer to a station a little closer to her mother.

"There is no Constabulary without its people," Ryan said, flatly.

He began steering her towards the door, conscious of the time.

"Look, Reed," he said, as they emerged out into the afternoon sunshine. "What if I were to arrange a transfer from the Alnwick station to our headquarters in town? You could work with Frank and me, and the rest of our team in Major Crimes. How would that be?"

Charlie was lost for words, and felt sudden tears burn the back of her eyes.

"That would be—sir, that would be wonderful. I can't tell you what a difference that would make for all of us."

Ryan held out his hand, and they shook on it.

"Consider it done," he said, and turned away to go in search of his wayward sergeant. "Safe driving, Reed—and remember, things can only get better."

Her lip wobbled. "Thank you again."

"You won't be thanking me when you're having to put up with Frank's shenanigans on a daily basis," he called back.

She smiled, and decided that one good turn deserved another. "He's in the clubhouse kitchen," she said. "There was leftover cake."

The air above Ryan's head turned blue and she beat a hasty retreat, in case there should be two crime scenes to investigate by the next morning.

Doctor Anna Taylor-Ryan heard the familiar sound of her husband's car pulling into their driveway, followed by the slamming of a car door and the crunch of his boots over the gravel as he made his way to the house. Things had never been the same since the privacy of their home was invaded a couple of years before, and for a long time afterwards she'd felt anxious every time a car pulled up, or whenever any unidentified noise disturbed the rural tranquil. Her arm wrapped a little more firmly around her daughter's waist as she watched an episode of *In the Night Garden*.

A moment later, the front door opened, and the fear in her chest melted away.

"Anna?"

"In here!" she called out.

Hearing him, Emma let out a delighted squeal and wriggled off her mother's lap to run towards the hallway and into her father's waiting arms.

"There, she is!" he exclaimed, lifting her up high.

"Hello, stranger," Anna said, and reached up to kiss him, then the back of Emma's head. "Just in time to help with bath time—or, should I say, 'splash time'?"

Emma favoured them both with a devilish smile that was, he had to admit, an exact replica of his own.

"Daddy needs a wash," she declared.

"Why does that feel like a threat?" he wondered aloud, and Anna laughed. "Come on, then. I'm ready to face my fate."

The three of them raced upstairs, and soon after there came a tidal wave of bubbly water from the family bathroom. As he and Anna sat together bathing their daughter, he couldn't help but think of Charlie Reed, who managed these moments alone.

"I'm going to take on a new member of the team," he told Anna. "Frank and I have worked with her before, on the case in Bamburgh, and she's got the right idea. Her name's Charlotte Reed, and she's got good instincts, professionalism, and a decent sense of humour, which is a must in our business."

Anna was surprised. "That's nice…but is it a bit soon after Mel's departure? Jack might think you're trying to replace her."

Ryan was ashamed to admit that he hadn't even considered that angle.

"Oh, sh—"

Anna looked pointedly at the little girl playing with a pair of rubber duckies, who was always listening.

"—*sugar*," he finished. "I hadn't thought of that."

"Well, I'm probably wrong," she said. "Jack's a grown man; I'm sure he'll understand."

"Are you kidding? He's over-sensitive about gluten and fast fashion," Ryan exclaimed. "He's going to blow a gasket, when he finds out."

"A gasket," Emma repeated, as if to rub salt into the wound.

"Look, I'll just explain that it's not about replacing Melanie, it's about plugging the resource gap in our team," he said, with a touch of desperation. "Besides, it does her a good turn, as well."

Anna was instantly concerned for the woman she'd never met. "Is she all right?"

"Charlie's a single mother, without much in the way of a support network," he explained. "Her own mother's about all she seems to have and, sadly, she's struck down with MS."

"Oh, that must be so hard," Anna said, and began thinking of ways to be a friend to Ryan's new team member. "Is there anything else we can do?"

Ryan leaned across to kiss her deeply.

"What was that for?" she asked softly.

"I just love you, that's all. I love that you feel compassion for all who need it," he said.

"Mwah-mwah!" Emma shouted, and they both turned to find their daughter sitting with her face upturned, indignation writ large.

"Nobody's forgetting you," Ryan laughed, and they both leaned down to administer the required dosage of kisses.

"All better," Emma declared, and went back to her ducks.

Once Ryan had sung the majority of Rodgers and Hammerstein's greatest hits, and particularly *The Sound of Music*, to Emma's satisfaction, he made his way back downstairs and into the kitchen, where Anna waited for him with a glass of wine and a plate of something hearty on the table.

"Just what the doctor ordered," he said, with an appreciative sniff.

"Thought you might be feeling peckish," she replied, and settled herself beside him.

She waited for him to swallow a few mouthfuls, then clinked her glass against his.

"How was your day?"

"Longer than expected," he replied. "Reed called us out to assess a body on the beach next to the Dunstanburgh Castle Golf Club, and these things always take longer than you think."

Anna smiled to herself and thought that, were it not for the fact she was the wife of a murder detective, she'd have no idea what to think about the process of managing a crime scene.

"I have a friend who lives up in Embleton," she said. "It's just around the corner from the golf club, the next bay along from Death Rocks.

Nothing ever really happens there, so I'm surprised there's been a murder."

"I'm fifty-fifty on whether this one will turn out to be homicide," he said. "A lot of the circumstantial evidence points to a nasty accident on the rocks, which are aptly named. But as for the general prospect of murders happening in small villages and towns, I think you and I both know, there's no greater hotbed of salacious gossip and criminal intent than in a small, rural parish. I'd sooner walk down a dark alleyway in the East End of London than face a crowd of villagers with pitchforks."

Anna laughed. "I sometimes wish I'd known you back when you were first cutting your teeth at the Met," she said, resting her head on her hand as she tried to imagine him as a younger man. "I suppose it's greedy to want to have known the person you love for as long as possible."

"Not really," he said. "I feel much the same way. I wonder how life would have been if I'd met you sooner."

"Neither of us were the same people we are now," she replied. "It's impossible to say."

"I was a 'work in progress'," he told her, and reached across to clasp her hand. "I needed those years without you to become a better man, so I would recognise when a better woman came along."

She smiled. "You can be quite poetic, sometimes."

Ryan shook his head, and took a sip of wine. "There's only one writer in this family," he said, and toasted his glass in her direction. "Have you decided whether to send your manuscript to a bunch of agents or just go ahead and publish independently?"

Anna had been published by academic publishing houses for several years, and her non-fiction tomes gathered dust on their family bookshelf and, most likely, on those at the student's library at Durham University, where she remained a senior lecturer. However, fiction was a totally different ball game, and she was the first to admit she was unsure of the correct road to take.

"I thought I might give the independent route a try but, before I do, it might be interesting to see what a selection of literary agents have to say," she replied. "I sent off a few query letters last week, so we'll see if any of them reply."

Ryan nodded, and sat back in his seat to look at her properly. "What if their feedback is negative?" he asked.

She shrugged. "What if the sky falls in?" she countered. "I'll cross that bridge when I come to it and, most likely, ignore it. The opinion of a single stranger doesn't matter to me half so much as yours."

Ryan lifted her hand to his lips, and kissed the underside of her wrist.

"And, more interestingly, what will you do if their feedback is *positive*?"

"I'll have to pluck up the courage and let people read my story, one way or another."

"Call me crazy, but that sounds even more terrifying than villagers with pitchforks and rampaging serial killers, combined," he quipped.

"Well, as Frank would say, I've always been a bit of a fruitcake."

"Aren't we all?"

"Must be the company we keep." She smiled, and polished off the last of her wine before changing the subject. "Hey, speaking of

Bamburgh…you remember the lovely old house where Angela lived?"

Ryan nodded, thinking of the beautiful old Georgian property with large sash windows and trailing ivy, across the road from the sand dunes and a stone's throw from Bamburgh Castle, which had once been home to the first kings of England.

"I certainly do," he said. "She was found dead there, remember?"

Anna waved that away as a trivial point.

"Well, I happened to notice it's been put up for sale," she said, very casually. "The new owner will have a lot of renovation work on their hands, but it'll be quite something when it's done."

Her words hung on the air for a few seconds, and then Ryan looked her dead in the eye.

"You thinking what I'm thinking?"

"Maybe…"

"The land where we built this place was my wedding present to you," he said, looking at the walls they'd built, and the view from the large windows overlooking the garden and the village of Elsdon beyond. "But that was before—"

"Yes," she said, quietly. "We've tried to get past it, Ryan, but they stole the feeling of safety I once felt living here. I can't bring it back."

He knew it, because he felt exactly the same.

"I had a thought, not so long ago, that this would make a lovely spot for Frank and Denise, especially since Samantha's horse is stabled at the bottom of the hill," Ryan said. "She could ride Pegasus all the time, rather than just visit on weekends."

"Do you think they'd want to live here?"

Ryan nodded. "Frank loves the place, and Denise was only saying last week they'd love to find somewhere like this," he replied. "I think it would be a bit outside their reach, but that's assuming we were to sell it on the open market. There's such a thing as 'mates rates', you know."

Anna smiled. "You thinking what I'm thinking?" she whispered.

"Maybe," he replied. "Let's set up a viewing of the property in Bamburgh."

"I'll call them, first thing tomorrow."

He raised a glass. "To the next chapter, and living by the sea."

"To the next chapter," she said, and clinked her empty glass against his. "And many more to come."

CHAPTER 9

The next morning

"Howay, man. Give us a break...my heart can't take much more of this..."

MacKenzie was merciless. "Eight more times," she told him.

Phillips was sweating at the thought. "*Eight*?" he squeaked. "Look, pet, you know I'd do anythin' for you, but—"

"Less talk, more action," she snapped.

Phillips' legs began to shake. "I—I don't know how much longer I can keep this up..." He wondered if it would be an unmanly thing to cry.

"*Three...two...one...and, relax.*"

MacKenzie and Phillips both collapsed onto their yoga mats, having performed a series of conditioning exercises designed to tighten their inner thighs. Their instructor was a professional dancer, with a professional dancer's approach to health and wellbeing, which was to accept nothing less than the best. Phillips might have admired her approach, if he hadn't found himself on the receiving end of it.

"Great work today," Melissa said. "Next week, we'll move onto the *hard* exercises."

Phillips gulped audibly.

"Denise, how did your bad leg feel, as we were doing those last reps?"

MacKenzie rubbed a hand over the bright blue leggings she wore, beneath which a long, faded scar was still visible against her pale skin. The man who'd put it there was no more, but he'd left his mark to ensure he'd never be forgotten.

"Right enough," she said, in her soft Irish burr. "It helps to keep active, so the muscles don't seize up."

"Remember to stretch it out. Frank? I think your form's getting better all the time."

It was lowering to admit it, but Phillips had always been susceptible to a bit of flattery.

"Well," he said, puffing out his chest a bit. "I was rememberin' what you said about hip rotation and all that."

Melissa exchanged a smile with Denise.

"I'm sure that'll have a range of benefits," she said, with a glint in her eye. "Maybe next time we should move on to some disco moves."

Unknowingly, she'd said the magic word.

"Disco?" he breathed.

"Frank," Denise tried to intervene. "Melissa's talking about some of the *stretches* you can do—"

But she was already too late.

"You've got The Hustle, of course," he said, ticking them off his fingers. "The Bus Stop, The Snap—and not forgettin' The Point Move. Last but not least…my personal favourite, The Funky Chicken."

Melissa blinked, momentarily lost for words.

"Now, a lot of people think they can do The Funky Chicken," he said, in a serious tone. "But if you don't get the elbows just right, you can do yourself an injury or what I like to call, 'Chicken Elbow'."

Melissa opened her mouth to say something, but Frank rolled on.

"If you need me to give you a few pointers, I could bring along my KC and the Sunshine Band CD."

Denise heaved a sigh that was part resignation, part amusement, while Melissa thought of the brand new remote-operated sound system she'd installed in her studio recently, no part of which required a compact disc.

Then, she thought of something better, and her mouth curved into a smile. "Frank, are you challenging me to a 'Dance Off'?"

Denise covered her face with her hands, not having anticipated there could be another living person who shared the same appreciation of the Funky Chicken, aside from her husband.

She'd never hear the end of it.

Phillips, meanwhile, was delighted. "Aye, I am! Bring on the 'turkey burn'—maybe we should call it the 'chicken burn' after this, eh?"

"You're on," Melissa laughed. "I'll see who else I can rope in—"

They both turned to Denise, who was too slow to run.

By the time he pulled up outside the service entrance at the Royal Victoria Infirmary, Phillips had already worked out much of the routine he planned to spring on his unsuspecting dance instructor, at the aforementioned Dance Off which had been scheduled for the end of the week. Admittedly, he'd need to dust off some of his old Ra-Ra-Rasputin squats, but he was fairly sure his gluteus maximus wouldn't let him down. He was still humming the song as he sashayed up to where Ryan stood, his long body leaning against one of the pillars outside the entrance as he held a mobile phone to his ear.

"—yes, go for it. I'll be there, if I can, so long as nothing comes up at work."

Phillips did a silent rendition of The Hustle, while Ryan tried to shoo him away with his free hand.

"What's that? No, it's just Frank, but I better get off now, it looks like he's having a fit." Ryan grinned at his sergeant's indignant face. "Love you, too." He rang off, and pocketed the phone.

"Your lovely wife, I take it?"

"Mm," Ryan replied, and pointed an accusatory finger. "Whatever happened to your 'poor old hip'?"

"It's a marvel what modern medicine and a good night's sleep can do."

"Uh huh. Come on, Twinkle Toes, let's see if the pathologist can shed any light on what happened to Will Harding."

"He's only had his body since yesterday afternoon," Phillips said, fairly.

"Long enough to give us the gist," Ryan said, as they descended into the bowels of the hospital. "I've never known Pinter to be wrong about his preliminary findings."

Phillips thought about it, and realised his friend was right. "Aye, you've gotta give it to him," he said. "Jeff knows the ins and outs of a dead body."

Ryan gave him the side-eye. "Bad puns aside, you seem remarkably chipper, this morning."

"It's the joys of Spring," Phillips declared, and breathed in deeply, an action he regretted immediately as his nostrils were filled with the unmistakeable, lingering scent of formaldehyde.

Presently, they reached a set of double doors, which required a key code for entry.

"Howay," Phillips said, after Ryan made no move to enter the code. "Don't tell me you've forgotten again."

"I haven't forgotten," Ryan hissed. "It's just temporarily slipped my mind."

Phillips raised an eyebrow. "Well, you know I never remember these things," he said, and rubbed the stubble on his chin which he'd missed while shaving that morning. "Last time, it was the year Freddie Mercury died, wasn't it?"

Ryan nodded.

"Before then, it was Whitney Houston," he muttered. "You might have guessed, he likes to commemorate the deaths of his favourite musicians."

"Do you remember what he was listening to when he changed the key code?"

"Oddly enough, I was busy during that momentous event," Ryan drawled. "But it's not a bad thought. Let's see…we've had Houston, Mercury, Lennon, Presley…"

He snapped his fingers, and keyed in four digits for "1997". "The Notorious B.I.G.," he provided, when the doors clicked open.

Phillips followed Ryan inside, and was distracted from their dismal surroundings by a vision of Jeff Pinter, their crusty, white, middle-aged pathologist, driving home wearing a durag.

Perish the thought...

The man himself popped his head around the side of an immersion tank, and waved a gloved hand dripping with something oozing and green.

"Be with you in a jiffy!"

"Take your time," they both said, with feeling.

They hovered beside the door, having availed themselves of a couple of visitors lab coats hanging on a hook just beside it, and trained their eyes on anything other than the cadaver that was currently being manhandled into the tank by Pinter and another member of staff.

"Look, when I go, just point me towards the sea, will you?" Phillips muttered. "I'm gannin' out like the Vikings did, on a burnin' raft to take us to Valhalla. I don't want any o' this proddin' and pokin' about."

"It's hardly as if you'll feel it, by then," Ryan was bound to say.

"All the same, I'm not havin' Pinter's bony hands all o'er my arse and God knows what else—"

Phillips' mouth snapped shut as the pathologist approached, thankfully having treated his bony hands to a thorough wash and a fresh pair of gloves.

"Good to see you both," he said.

"Aye, you too," Phillips said, blandly. "How's tricks?"

"Trickier than usual," Pinter surprised him by saying. "We've had an unprecedented number of cases coming through the doors this past winter—that's why I'm in on a Sunday."

Ryan frowned slightly, because he'd been thinking recently that the number of fatalities was significantly higher than in the previous year.

"Any pattern to it?" he asked.

Pinter sighed expansively, then shook his head.

"Nothing obvious," he replied. "Just a collection of accidents and manslaughters, which you're already aware of. None of the injuries or circumstances have been alike, and I can't see any obvious connection between them, so it's just one of those things."

Ryan told himself not to look for shadows when there were none to be found; it was a bad occupational hazard.

"In that case, let's talk about Will Harding," he said. "Have you had a chance to take a look at him?"

"Ah, yes, the young man who arrived yesterday," Pinter said, and prepared to launch into one of his mini lectures. "Now, you *know* I need an adequate amount of time to be able to produce a meaningful report—"

"I do," Ryan cut in, adopting a suitably deferential tone. "In fact, Frank and I were just saying, we wouldn't *dream* of relying on anything you hadn't put your signature to, but, knowing that you're an expert in your field, we've always benefited from an early steer from you. Isn't that right, Frank?"

Phillips looked at his friend as if he'd grown two heads. "Er...aye?"

"Well," Pinter relented, "I suppose I could give you some early observations, since you're here. Follow me, I've put him in one of the examination rooms this way."

He led them from the main, open plan space through a side door leading to a number of smaller, private examination rooms which tended to be reserved for those cadavers which had seen more trauma than most, or otherwise needed special handling.

"Here we are," Pinter announced, and swiped a key card to open a door marked

'EXAMINATION ROOM C'. "I'm sure I don't need to warn you, but this one makes for difficult viewing."

Phillips knew that, for a pathologist to issue that kind of warning, it must be bad.

"I'll just—take the weight off my feet—" he mumbled, and made a dive for the office chair parked beside the long desk in the corner of the room, as far away from the action as possible.

"Frank, for pity's sake, why do you bother coming along if you're planning to hide away in the corner?" Ryan asked.

"I'm not *hidin'*," Phillips said, in dignified tones. "I can see perfectly well from here, that's all."

"It must be almost twenty-five years that we've known one another," Pinter said, with a touch of nostalgia. "Even longer than this feller's been in the North"—he bobbed his head towards Ryan—"and, in all that time, I have to give you credit for never once losing the contents of your stomach, Frank. I can't tell you how many young rookies come through those doors and throw up all over the floor."

It was high praise from a man like Pinter.

"*Thank* you, Jeff," Phillips said, with a pointed look at Ryan, who folded his arms across his chest. "It's been touch and go, at times."

"I'll be touching you with the business end of my boot, if you don't watch it," Ryan muttered. "Now, can we talk about how this man died?"

Pinter chuckled, and moved across to one of the cold storage compartments, whereupon he retrieved the body of what had once been a man. He wheeled the gurney into the centre of the room, and, after a moment's pause to allow the others to prepare themselves, turned back the covering.

Phillips sucked the air between his teeth, and focused on the heavy-duty linoleum flooring, while Ryan stared at the image until his body righted itself and he was able to speak.

"I saw him on the beach, yesterday," he said quietly. "But there's something about seeing them laid out on a cold slab...he looks like a waxwork model, without eyes."

Pinter seldom revealed much about his finer feelings towards the dead in his charge, but, that day, he made an exception. "I have the opposite problem," he said, and the other two turned to him in surprise. "You have to tell yourself not to feel too much, to stay detached so that you can carry out your investigation, don't you?"

They nodded.

"I was like that, for the first few years," he said. "I used to go home and feel sick; I'd have nightmares, imagining their faces looming over me in the night—"

"I never knew that, Jeff," Phillips said, and tried to reconcile the idea of him being as human as the rest of them.

Pinter gave a self-conscious shrug. "Of course," he said. "But, as time has worn on, I think you become desensitized to seeing the cadavers. Nothing is a surprise, anymore, and handling the bodies every day has slowly removed any fear I might have had, at first. They're just casings, shells, or whatever you want to call them. They're like frames without the paintings inside."

It was an apt description, Ryan thought.

"As a clinician, a degree of detachment is imperative," Pinter continued. "But, as I said at the beginning, I have the opposite problem to you both. Sometimes, I fear I've become too detached. I have to remind myself, at the start of every day, to treat each new visitor as if they were a customer in my shop; I have to care about how they would rate my service, if they were able to. I want their families to know I did all I could for them, and cared for the physical remains of the person they used to be, because they mattered to someone—even if they, themselves, had behaved badly."

"We have the same conflict when we're avenging the dead," Ryan said. "Not every victim is a paragon, but we have to treat them equally, in terms of how we investigate their murder."

Pinter nodded. "Some are easier than others," he said, and left it at that.

Ryan was about to move on, before remembering that Jeff Pinter had been the man to care for his sister's body, as well as that of her killer, Keir Edwards. At the time, he'd been so focused on his own grief, his own heartache and pain, he hadn't stopped to imagine how difficult a task that must have been for the quiet, lonely man who did such important work.

"Thank you, Jeff," he said. "For everything."

Pinter looked up in surprise, then mild embarrassment, before understanding all that Ryan had left unsaid.

"Don't mention it," he said, and then cleared his throat. "Now, as you can see, we've got a male, aged twenty-eight, according to his official records. Aside from his present condition, Will Harding was in very good health when he was alive. I've sent over the usual hair and blood samples for testing, but, judging from the overall BMI, the muscle mass, the general state of his teeth and gums and so forth, I'd say he was in peak physical condition—in fact, he was hoping for a feature in *Men's Health*, if that six pack is anything to go by."

"Y' see, now, this is the mistake these young lads are makin'," Phillips piped up, from the back. "Sometimes, you need a bit of cushioning to be able to fight off an attacker," he argued, and tapped his own rapidly shrinking paunch. "Besides which, it gives the lasses somethin' to hold on to." He winked at them both.

"Well, sadly for this gentleman, body mass would have made no difference to the eventual outcome," Pinter said, and used a retractable pointer to indicate a large cavity on the back of Harding's skull. "He was struck from behind, so he wouldn't have had any opportunity to react."

"Struck?" Ryan queried. "You don't think he fell?"

Pinter shook his head decisively. "Not in the way you mean," he replied. "When we trip over something, our natural reflex is to put our hands out to break the fall."

He pointed towards Harding's hands, which were covered in two clear plastic bags that were slowly inflating with natural gases.

"His hands show no sign of abrasion, other than the usual hardened skin you'd expect from repetitive action, such as operating a camera. That makes it very unlikely that he fell while he was conscious. It's far more likely he was struck from behind and fell forward, so was unable to make any attempt to break the fall. That would explain the fracture in his right knee, the abrasion on his forehead, and the breakage in his nose."

"Any idea what kind of implement might have been used?"

"Any heavy blunt object would have done it; a marble ashtray, if people still smoked these days, or that sort of thing—"

"What about a golf club?" Phillips suggested, from the back of the room. "Heavy metal, easy to swing…seems perfect for the job."

"My thoughts, exactly," Ryan said.

"That would certainly fit the bill, so long as it was a driver rather than a putter or an iron," came the reply. "We're looking for something roundish, rather than anything with a bevelled edge. We'll test the skin around the site and inside the wound for any traces of metal or other compounds that could give us a clue as to the weapon."

Ryan turned to Phillips. "Let's get a warrant to seize all the clubs we can get our hands on," he said. "Faulkner can test for DNA."

Phillips nodded, and made a note to get the process underway. "Could have been one of the rocks," he pointed out. "They'd be heavy enough to cave someone's head in."

"Faulkner hasn't found any with blood or brain matter," Ryan replied. "Besides which, I don't think Harding died on the beach, did he?"

This last question was directed at Pinter, who smiled and shook his head. "I'd be very surprised if he did," came the reply. "For one thing, it's evident from the extensive livor mortis you can see on Harding's face and the anterior parts of his body, that he lay on his front for some considerable time after he died—at least a couple of hours, I'd say."

"Whereas we found him lying on his back," Ryan said. "No obvious blood loss around him, no other sign that it was a kill site."

"So, whoever killed him then moved him, to make it look more like an accident?" Phillips said, and cursed himself for catching sight of the dead man's feet, which had come loose from the cotton shroud.

"That has to be the working theory," Ryan agreed. "Do you have any idea of post-mortem interval, Jeff?"

"I'd approximate his time of death to be somewhere between ten o'clock on Friday night, and one o'clock Saturday morning."

"The Club Secretary, Dawson, said he last clocked Harding chattin' up that barmaid, Molly Whatsherface, at the clubhouse bar at around ten-thirty," Phillips recalled. "If he's right, we can narrow that timescale a bit."

Ryan nodded. "We can work with that," he said, with more confidence than he felt. "Thanks, Jeff."

They talked for a short while longer, and then made for the door. Before they could turn the handle, Pinter remembered another thing he'd meant to tell them.

"Before you go, I wanted to give you an update about another case."

They waited, aware that he enjoyed the pageantry of it all.

"Atherton—Marcus, I think? First came to me three or four months ago."

Ryan's ears pricked. "Yes, that's the one. What about him?"

"MacKenzie asked for an extended toxicology report, which, unfortunately, was compromised the first time we sent it off," he replied. "These things happen, when you have to send samples to an outside lab." He tutted. "Anyway, we sent off a second round for testing, and the results have finally come back. Although Atherton died of carbon monoxide poisoning, the results show that there was another unidentified organic compound in his bloodstream at the time of death. It doesn't match any of the usual compounds, so that's a bit of a puzzle. I thought you'd want to know."

Ryan nodded his thanks. "That's good news," he said.

"It is?"

"Yep," he said, cheerfully. "Yesterday, we had no new leads, and today, we do. That's a good news day."

"Takes all sorts," Phillips muttered to Pinter, as they left.

CHAPTER 10

At roughly the same time Phillips had been feeling his thighs burn, Jack Lowerson pulled into the car park at the Dunstanburgh Castle Golf Club. There were only a couple of other cars parked there, one of which he recognised as Faulkner's van and, since he knew the victim's car had already been towed the previous day, he assumed the remaining vehicle belonged to a member of the golf club. It was early still, and he sat quietly in the driver's seat for long minutes watching the sun blaze into life, first in pastel shades of purple and pink, which melted gradually into a wash of deep, fiery ochre that licked the walls of Dunstanburgh Castle like flames, as though it were under siege in times of old.

Melanie would have loved to see this, came the unbidden thought.

Angry with himself, and with her, Jack was about to reach for a jacket lying on the passenger seat when he caught sight of movement in his peripheral vision.

Through the windshield, he watched a slim woman of around his own age step out of a small red Fiat, balancing a cup of takeaway coffee in one hand and a slim file in the other. She wore blue jeans, boots and a smart navy jacket, while her mid-brown hair was pulled back into a simple ponytail. To his surprise—and irritation—she began to walk across the car park towards him, an action which drew attention to the long line of her legs and the quiet, understated attractiveness of her face, which was schooled into a friendly, open smile.

Since he made no move to get out of his own vehicle, she tapped her knuckle against the side of his window, which he lowered with some reluctance.

"Hello," she said. "You must be DC Lowerson?"

Jack scowled at her. "Yes?"

"DC Reed," she said. "From the Alnwick office. I was the first responder, yesterday, and I've been working with Ryan and Phillips. I had a message to say you'd be on your way up here, today, so I thought I'd pop across and introduce myself."

Lowerson looked at her with a measure of suspicion that was entirely of his own making. When he'd received a message from Ryan to say they were working with a local DC by the name of Charlie Reed, he'd assumed it was some backwater bloke whose bread and butter consisted of breaking up fights outside the local pub.

"Right," he muttered, and made a grab for his coat. "Mind out of the way."

Charlie stepped back, so he could unfold himself from the car.

"Um," she said, scrambling for an icebreaker. "Do you want me to bring you up to speed with the progress that's been made?"

"I read Ryan's summary note," he said. "But tell me if you want."

Not the most encouraging introduction, she thought, but perhaps he wasn't much of a morning person.

"Would you like a coffee?" she asked him. "Or a bacon sandwich?"

"I'm vegetarian," he said, peevishly, and instantly hated himself for being so rude. "But… thanks for the offer."

She kept the smile on her face, but some of the light had faded from her eyes, and her mind categorised him as being precisely the kind of rude, arrogant individual she would never befriend, let alone work with, unless she had no choice in the matter.

Such as now.

"Well," she said, injecting as much positivity into the statement as she could muster. "I'm looking forward to working with you. What was your first name, again?"

He began walking towards the clubhouse, and she kept pace with him.

"Jack," he muttered.

"Call me Charlie," she offered, since he didn't ask. "I'm looking forward to working with you, Jack."

"It'll only be a few days," he said, mostly to himself. "We'll wrap up the scene here as quickly as we can."

She frowned, and shook her head. "No…I meant, I'm looking forward to working with you in Major Crimes. Ryan offered me a transfer, and I've accepted. If he and Frank are anything to go by, it'll be a riot—"

"Sorry," he interrupted her, and came to a shuddering halt on the asphalt. "Did you say you're transferring to *our* team?"

"Yes," she said, and her tone hardened, just a fraction. "Do you have a problem with that?"

"Apparently not," he said, between gritted teeth. "It seems we're all expendable."

With that last damning statement, he left her standing there and strode towards the main doors of the clubhouse, only to find them locked from the night before.

She jangled a set of keys. "These might help," she said, mildly.

If looks could have killed, she thought, Jack would have murdered her on the spot.

Luckily for her, she was made of tougher stuff. "Mind out of the way," she said, sweetly.

By the time Ryan and Phillips made it back to Dunstanburgh, they could have sworn the temperature had fallen to somewhere below zero, if the atmosphere inside the clubhouse was anything to go by.

"It's worse than Pinter's gaff, in here," Phillips said, and nodded towards Lowerson and Reed, who stood on the far side of the function room facing one another, arms folded, in a classic stand-off.

"I'm going to go out on a limb here, and guess that Jack's found out Charlie's going to be joining us," Ryan said. "I was hoping to be able to tell him myself, but I haven't had a chance."

"Well, there's no reason for him to get all huffy about it," Phillips said. "Being angry about a new member on the team isn't going to bring Mel back, is it?"

Ryan shook his head. "If and when Mel returns, she has a desk ready and waiting for her," he said. "Until then, we can always use a good officer with a nose for the business, and I believe in rewarding hard work."

"Aye, you've always been good at talent spottin'," Phillips said.

"I don't need to be any kind of expert to pick up on the signals here," Ryan muttered, having made a brief survey of the body language between Jack and Charlie. "I hope this isn't going to be a problem, because I've already got one toddler at home; I don't need any more tears or tantrums at work."

Phillips pulled an expressive face. "Aye, well, I've got a teenager and that's not much better," he said. "I can't decide which is worse, but I'm with you, lad."

They breathed in a synchronised breath, and let it out again.

"Ready?" Phillips asked him.

"Always," Ryan said, and pushed through the doors. "Morning! Jack, Charlie...I see you've already introduced yourselves."

Lowerson looked mutinous. "*Yes*, DC Reed has informed me she'll be joining our team in Newcastle."

"Well, I hope you gave her a friendly welcome," came the swift rejoinder.

Lowerson opened his mouth, but whatever acidic remark he'd planned to say was intercepted in the nick of time.

"Oh, *yes*," Charlie said, surprising them all. "Jack has been very kind, telling me all about what to expect from my new team." She turned to him with a bland smile. "He's even offered to help me move house," she added, and thought she heard him utter a strangled gasp. "I'm blown away by his kindness."

Ryan mentally applauded her, but wasn't fooled for a moment. "I'd expect nothing less," he said, and looked Jack squarely in the eye so that he might read the unspoken warning in his own.

"Well, then!" Phillips exclaimed, clapping his hands together. "Let's get down to business. We've just come from the pathologist's office, and he's of the same opinion as us, which is that—"

"A rabbit's off?" Reed put in, to make him laugh.

"Exactly!" Phillips chuckled. "See? You catch on, quick."

Watching their byplay, Lowerson was even more incensed that, in less than twenty-four hours, Charlie Reed had already tapped into their team banter and, worse still, was actively participating in it.

The nerve.

"All things point to Mr Harding having been killed somewhere other than where we found him," Ryan said, and leaned against the back of one of the tub chairs upholstered in wipe-clean, bottle green pleather. "Faulkner's team haven't been able to find any obvious 'fall' site to correspond with the idea of an accidental death, so Pinter's opinion adds weight to the idea that Harding died elsewhere, and was moved to that spot on the beach sometime during the early hours of yesterday morning."

"What time does the pathologist think he died?" Reed asked.

"We're looking at a window of between ten-thirty on Friday evening, and two o'clock on Saturday morning," he replied. "Given there was a party underway, I'd guess Harding was killed somewhere on site, and was then moved once everyone had gone home, under cover of darkness. That's always assuming he was murdered by someone at the party, of course."

"It's possible he could have made plans to meet someone in the area, then slipped out of the party unnoticed," Lowerson said. "We don't know enough about the victim's communications history before the event, and we haven't completed the mammoth task of interviewing everyone who came along to the retirement party. We may have an ever-wider field to cover."

"That's very true," Ryan agreed, and was pleased his young friend had recovered his professionalism, at least for the time being.

He turned to their newest recruit. "Did the Club Secretary provide you with that list of attendees?"

Reed nodded, and handed over a copy from the file she kept tucked beneath her arm.

"As you'll see, there are a hundred and thirty-two names listed as invited guests, not including two bar staff on loan from the pub in the Embleton; a DJ by the name of "DJ Dangerman"; four catering staff provided by the catering company from Craster; a local magician by the name of 'Magic Trevor"; and, of course, the photographer and suspected victim, Will Harding."

"Which makes a total of one hundred and forty potential witnesses at the party," Ryan calculated. "I suppose it could be worse."

"Could be a stadium of spectators," Phillips said. "I'm dreadin' the day someone pops their clogs on the pitch at St. James' Park, because it would be muggins here who'd have to speak to them all."

"You'd be up to the Executive Suite faster than a mountain goat," Ryan said. "In fact, I'm surprised you haven't paid a hitman to bump someone off, just so you'd have an excuse to get a selfie with the team."

"That's not a bad idea."

Ryan flashed a smile. "We need to narrow the pool," he said. "Nothing on Harding's phone was suspicious. The last communication he received was a text from Molly, the barmaid, who was evidently dropping him a line so he'd have her number for use at a later date. Before then, he had a few messages from John Dawson with details of where to park and how to get to the clubhouse, which came after an exchange of messages a few weeks prior to the event, obviously confirming details of their agreement and what he would be expected to capture on film. All of it was completely normal. He had messages from his mother that were quite sweet, a few from his father about football and whether he wanted to try and catch the match next Saturday, as well as several from other unknown women which were—"

"Downright *filthy*," Phillips put in, outraged. "I don't want to *think* what their da's would say, if they knew the muck that was being sent back and forth—"

"I'm surprised you weren't taking notes," Ryan joked.

"I don't need any help speakin' the Language of Love," Phillips shot back, with a wink for the others. "Seems like Will Harding wasn't too bad himself, judging by the number of lasses he had on the go. I'm only surprised he wasn't dizzy."

"In that case, let's hope we're not looking for a jealous husband," Ryan said. "Aside from the text messages, he had a couple of voicemail messages from potential clients, more enquiries via the Messenger app on his phone, but that's as far as we've got. Digital Forensics have his devices, including his laptop—which was actually in the boot of his car—and will be looking to see if anything's been deleted. They'll take a dive into his social accounts, e-mail and so on, and if we come across anything else during the search of his flat, later today, we'll add that to the list and we'll just have to wait and see if anything gets thrown up. For the time being, let's assume someone present here last night had reason to kill him, and focus our efforts on trying to narrow the pool of suspects."

"For starters, nobody at the party went missing for any extended period of time," Lowerson said. "We've had a look at the CCTV footage covering the car park last night, and there were an occasional few who stepped outside to have a cigarette or a vape, but they came in again afterwards and were mostly joined by at least one other person at all times. Nobody smoked alone or wandered off. There was a small camera overlooking the bar area, but it's very old and the footage is grainy. With a bit of effort, we can identify the faces, but it does confirm Dawson's statement that Harding was at the bar, chatting with Molly Finch, until ten-thirty-seven on Friday evening. After then, we don't know where he went—yet."

Ryan nodded. "That's good work, both of you. See if you can get your hands on any CCTV footage from the village," he said, thinking of nearby Embleton, which was the only road access to the club since the route via Craster and Dunstanburgh Castle could only be taken by foot. "Better ask National Heritage for any footage they have from their end, and check with the holiday cottage which sits nearest to the entrance of the footpath leading from Craster to the castle. If anyone was going to take a circuitous route, they'd have to go past it, so let's see if we get lucky. Perhaps we can look for any unidentified vehicles approaching, later in the evening, or rule out the possibility."

Lowerson and Reed nodded, in unison.

"Dawson has also told us that he doesn't think Harding knew anyone at the party," Charlie said, thoughtfully. "I think it's worth speaking to Molly, to find out what they talked about, and see if that rings true."

"Good plan," Ryan approved. "You do that, and take Jack with you. After you've spoken with her, start making your way down the list of party-goers, and find out whatever you can, specifically if they remember seeing Harding at any point in the evening. See if any of them have footage or pictures of last night's event and, if so, ask them to send it to us so we can go through the images to see if Harding's in any of them. If he is, we can check the time stamps and perhaps narrow the time of death even further."

"All right," she said, and turned to the man standing a safe distance away from her. "Shall we hit the road, Jack?"

With one last, fulminating glare, Lowerson followed her from the room.

Once they were safely out of earshot, Phillips let out a hearty chuckle and turned to his friend. "We could ask a few of the local bobbies to go down that list of attendees," he said. "It's not strictly necessary for the pair o' them to do the legwork."

"Oh, yes it is," Ryan said. "They need to learn to play nicely together, and what better way than being forced to conduct a series of monotonous interviews with a bunch of local golfers who'll probably talk *about* golfing?"

"You speak as though golfing is a boring pastime," Phillips said, conversationally.

"Whatever gave you that impression?"

"Nowt much; just your tone, demeanour, and choice of language."

"I always said you were a master detective." With that, he pushed away from his chair and began walking towards the utility corridor which led to the kitchen, cloakrooms and the service entrance.

"Where are you off to now?"

He paused, and turned back to his friend. "I was just thinking, if I were a killer looking to move a body from here to the thirteenth hole, what would be the best way of doing that?"

The penny dropped.

"Golf buggy," Phillips said.

"Exactly."

CHAPTER 11

"Jack? Do you mind if I have a word?"

Lowerson slowed, but did not stop walking along the windy road leading from the golf course towards the pretty village of Embleton. "I have a feeling I don't have a choice in the matter," he said.

"Your feeling is correct," she said, and grabbed his arm to pull him to a halt.

He leapt backwards, as though she'd burned him.

"Sorry," she said, and held up her hands. "I hope I didn't hurt you—"

"You didn't," he said shortly. "What do you want to talk about?" Impatience was written in every line of his body, which was encased in form-fitting jeans and a ski jacket.

"Look, you're obviously not happy that I'm going to be joining your team," she began, and tried not to feel hurt by it. "I don't know what I've done to offend you, but, if you'll tell me, I'll do what I can to fix it."

Within reason, she added silently.

Lowerson felt a small stab of guilt. "It's not... *you*, as such," he said, and stuck his hands in his pockets, feeling awkward.

Charlie sighed. "I've trodden on some toes, haven't I?" she whispered. "I didn't mean to, but I have. Is that it?"

He didn't see any point in lying to her, so he nodded. "My girlfriend, Melanie, went through a bad time last year," he said, averting his gaze from hers, which was just too kind. "She's taken a sabbatical from the team, to give herself time to heal from it. I always thought...I suppose I didn't think Ryan would fill her chair so quickly."

The 'old' Charlie might have suggested she cancel the transfer, or some such foolish thing, to appease his feelings, but the 'new', stronger Charlie couldn't afford to look a gift horse in the mouth. She was sorry for his loss, for that was what it was, but she had a family to consider and had worked hard enough to earn her place on Ryan's team, just as he had.

"I'm sorry you feel that way," she said, and that was true enough. "I hope your girlfriend recovers as soon as possible." She chose her next words with care. "That being said, I want to be clear about something. I'm not filling anyone else's chair, Jack. I'm pulling up my *own*. I'm nobody's substitute, and never will be."

He swallowed, and looked away, out towards the sea.

"I hope to meet Melanie, one day," she added. "She must be a saint for putting up with you, so maybe she can give me some pointers."

His head whipped back around, and a smile crept onto his face.

"Shall we start again?" he offered, after a short, tense moment. "I'm Jack Lowerson. Detective Constable—and Prize Idiot."

Reed grinned broadly, and took the hand he held out to her.

"Charlie," she smiled.

Molly Finch was a nineteen-year-old drama student, who lived with her family in Embleton and occasionally worked as a barmaid in her local pub or at the golf club. When she wasn't doing either of those things, she supplemented her income through a series of affiliate partnerships as a social media influencer, flogging hair and beauty products to a growing list of online followers who believed she was an up-and-coming young starlet with skin like a peach thanks to an extensive—and expensive—skincare regime.

When Jack and Charlie arrived at the white-painted bungalow where she lived, they interrupted a livestream report she happened to be broadcasting to thousands of strangers, in which she was telling them how thankful she was to have a full-coverage concealer to hide the ravages of a sleepless night.

"—and, honestly, I'm *obsessed* with this lipstick, in shade 005, 'Midnight Temptress'," she carried on. "It really complements my skin, which is paler than usual today—"

"Molly? There are a couple of police officers here to speak with you!"

Furious at the interruption, her daughter ended the livestream with the jab of one long fingernail and stomped towards her bedroom door.

"Mam! I've told you not to interrupt me when I'm filming—" Her tirade came to an abrupt end when she saw the two strangers standing behind her.

"They've come to speak to you about that lad who died," her mother said, anxiously.

Molly made a leisurely assessment of Jack, and found him to her taste.

"*Hi*," she beamed at him, ignoring Charlie completely. "Um, let's go into the lounge, shall we? Would you like a drink?"

"No, thanks," Reed said, tartly. "We don't have a lot of time, Ms Finch, so we'd like to get straight down to it."

Molly wasn't accustomed to being told what to do, and she didn't like it one little bit.

On the other hand, her mamma hadn't raised a quitter.

"Of course," she said, and raised wide, baby-blue eyes towards Jack. "I felt *terrible*, when I heard what had happened to Will. It's awful to think that, just a few hours before, he was offering to take some head shots for me."

She waited, expectantly.

"Head shots?" Lowerson queried, and she preened a bit.

"Yeah, I need them for when I'm auditioning or to put on my agent's website," she explained, and didn't bother to mention that she hadn't yet found an agent. "Anyway, Will and I got chatting, and he said he'd take them for free."

Nothing in life was free, Charlie thought, but having a care for the girl's mother who was seated on the sofa beside her daughter, didn't bother to press the point.

"Around what time were you chatting with Mr Harding?" she asked, although they already knew the answer from the CCTV footage.

"Hm…I'm not exactly sure, but it must have been quite late in the evening, because everyone had eaten their dinner and most of them were on the dance floor by then," Molly replied. "I'd guess around ten o'clock…maybe a bit later?"

Close enough, Charlie thought.

"Do you remember what you talked about?" Jack asked, and Molly gave him her full attention once more.

"Oh, you know, this and that," she said, and flipped her hair over her shoulder. "He asked if he'd seen me somewhere before, because he was sure he'd seen me on the telly or in a magazine."

Charlie caught Jack's eye, and found he, too, was hiding a smile. Phillips had been right about Will Harding being a talented linguist in the Language of Love.

"He must have thought I was an actress or a model," Molly said, to really drive home the point. "He said he'd worked with a lot of wannabes but, every now and then, he'd come across someone who had star quality."

"Aside from discussing your, ah…*career*, did Mr Harding talk about anything else?"

"He said he was going to take me to the House of Tides," she said, naming a Michelin-starred restaurant down by the Quayside in Newcastle. It was an expensive, if delicious, choice for a first date, and left Jack wondering how the late Mr Harding could afford it, especially if he was in the habit of wining and dining every one of his women in a similar fashion.

He made a note to ask about Harding's circumstances.

"Sounds nice," he said, lightly. "Anything else?"

Molly pouted a bit, feeling put out that her efforts to inveigle the young detective constable were obviously falling flat.

"I dunno," she said, crossing her legs. "He said he was celebrating a good start to the year, so we'd make a real night of it. I gave him my number, and then a bunch of people came up to the bar, so I had to get back to work. I didn't see him, after that."

She didn't sound especially upset about the implications of that, except perhaps to feel annoyed that she'd have to pay for her own head shots now.

"He didn't talk about anything that was worrying him, or mention anything that had upset him?" Reed asked, but Molly shook her head.

"Not that I remember," she said. "Why are you asking me all these questions, anyway? I thought he fell on the beach?"

"We like to have a complete picture," Jack said, and, at Charlie's nod, they rose to their feet and prepared to leave. "If you remember anything else, please get in touch."

Once they stepped back out into the morning air, Jack and Charlie waited until they'd cleared the house before passing any comment.

"You know," she said, thoughtfully. "When I first met you, I wondered if I'd seen you somewhere before…"

Jack burst out laughing. "You offering to pay for some head shots?"

"Nope," she said. "I've just realised where I actually *have* seen you before. The Northumbria Police Constabulary's Charity Christmas Calendar—"

Lowerson swore, volubly. "For the record, I was coerced into being 'Mr July' against my better judgment."

"Aww," she said. "I thought the inflatable pineapple ring was a nice touch."

He glared at her.

"Can I get your autograph?" she crooned.

"Shut it, Reed."

Her laughter sang through the streets of Embleton and, for the first time in weeks, he found himself laughing, too.

CHAPTER 12

As the sun dipped lower in the sky, Ryan and Phillips left the clubhouse in the capable hands of Faulkner's team of forensic staff and made their way back towards the city of Newcastle. Will Harding had recently moved into a new apartment and, to Ryan's dismay, it turned out to be in the same building where he had once lived, and where his sister had died.

"You alreet doin' this, son?" Phillips' quiet voice broke into the silence, and Ryan nodded, not taking his eyes from the road ahead.

"I'm fine, Frank."

His sergeant wasn't convinced. "I know it's been a few years, but nobody could blame you for feeling a bit raw, still. It's understandable."

Ryan nodded, and smiled across at his friend. "Honestly, I'll be fine. It isn't the same apartment, for one thing, and it's only bricks and mortar, after all."

Phillips didn't argue further, but kept a watchful eye on his friend as they made their way through the streets of the city towards the river, where a smart apartment complex overlooked the water. There was an underground car park for residents, where Ryan had once parked his car every night, but this time he found a spot in a side street not far away and turned off the engine.

"You're right, Frank," he said, after a minute. "It is hard."

"You don't have to go inside," his friend said quietly. "You don't have anythin' to prove to me, son."

Ryan leaned his head back against the headrest. "Ten years," he whispered. "It feels like yesterday. I can remember the last time I saw her…and I remember how he looked, when…"

"Don't think of it," Phillips advised. "Some things are best left to the past."

Ryan looked across at him, and his eyes were dark with emotion. "I don't ever want to hide from shadows," he said. "If I don't go inside now, I'll always know the spectre of Keir Edwards beat me, even though he's dead and gone. I won't allow it."

Phillips nodded slowly. "I'll be with you," he said. "Any time you want to leave, we will."

Ryan tapped the steering wheel, decisively. "Let's get it over with," he said, and prepared to face the past.

"It hasn't changed much."

Ryan made this observation as they entered the wide marble and glass foyer of his old apartment building, where he stood for a moment looking around the walls of a place that had once been a big part of his life.

"Can I help you?"

A concierge was seated behind a small reception desk, but it was not the same old gentleman who'd once greeted him every day, for Harry had passed away two or three years before; Ryan knew, because he'd sent flowers for his family.

"DCI Ryan and DS Phillips, Northumbria CID," he said, and they produced their warrant cards for inspection. "Unfortunately, we're investigating the death of one of your residents here—Will Harding, who lives in 3B."

The concierge, Shahid Malik, was shocked. "*Will?*" he cried. "But…I only saw him on Friday. Are you sure he's dead?"

"Well, if he isn't, he's givin' a good impression of it," Phillips said, and leaned in for a cosy chat. "You say you last saw him on Friday, eh?"

Malik nodded, looking between the pair of them. "I—yes, yeah. I saw him on Friday, must've been around lunchtime. He was heading out, and had his camera bag with him. I asked him where he was off to, and he said he had a job up on the coast somewhere, but he had a few errands to run, first."

"Did he say what those errands were?" Ryan asked.

Malik shook his head. "No, but he looked happy enough," he said. "In fact, he looked pretty chuffed with himself. I put it down to the fact he'd come home with a lass the night before."

"Did you catch her name?"

Malik shook his head again. "They don't usually stop to chat," he said. "I can tell you she was about twenty-one or thereabouts, pretty with long blonde hair, but that's about it."

"Fair enough," Phillips said. "D' you happen to know if he's had any visitors lately, other than the usual stream of lady friends? Any trouble from anyone?"

Malik looked surprised. "Trouble? No, nothin' like that," he said. "He always had a smile on his face, even when things were a bit slow."

They thanked him, and were about to head over to the lift that would take them to the third floor, when Ryan thought of something else. He turned back to the concierge.

"One last question, for now," he said, and the man spread his hands in an open gesture.

"Happy to help, if I can."

"You said that things had been slow for Will, from time to time—is that right?"

"Seemed that way to me," Malik replied. "At least, he never seemed to be working much."

Ryan knew from his own experience that the building wasn't cheap, which begged the question of how Harding could afford to live there without a regular stream of income.

He made a mental note to visit the man's family and look into his financial situation.

"Okay," he said. "Thanks for your help."

"Any time."

A few minutes later, Ryan reiterated his mental note.

He stood on the plush carpet floor of Harding's bedroom, which was pristine and decorated in monochromatic shades of white and grey. Gadgetry was everywhere, from voice activated lighting and speakers, to hidden TV screens behind mirrors and pictures in almost every room, and an entire cupboard full of cameras and accessories.

But it was the man's dressing room that clinched it.

Two banks of fancy built-in cupboards heaved with clothing and shoes, many still with the tags on, as well as a drawer full of premium watches, belts and ties. Yet another area boasted an array of trendy sportswear, some of which looked to be limited edition, signed by some sporting star or another.

"Bloody Nora, who did he think he was? A Saudi prince?" Phillips exclaimed, upon entering the room behind Ryan. "I've never seen so many togs outside of a department store."

"He liked some of the finer things, that's for sure. I'm not entirely sure how he could have afforded them, though."

"Rich family?" Phillips wondered aloud.

"No idea," Ryan said. "I thought we'd pay them a visit, after we're done here."

Frank read his mind with ease. "You're thinkin' he had a little side hustle? Maybe dealin' some drugs?"

Ryan inclined his head. "It wouldn't be the first time," he said. "It would explain how he could live this kind of lifestyle on his salary. He might have been a good photographer, but it was never going to make him millions."

Phillips agreed. "If he was dealin' on the side, that puts a different complexion on things," he said. "Could be he managed to annoy a supplier, or many a thing."

"True, but gangs don't tend to bother with staging bodies neatly on the beach after golf retirement parties," he said. "If anything, they'd want to send a message."

Phillips made a murmuring sound of agreement.

"Well, let's look at what we know," he said. "There's been no forced entry in here, has there?"

Ryan shook his head. "Nope, the lock is intact," he said. "We used the keys that were found inside Harding's coat pocket to access the flat, and Malik's got a second set downstairs for emergencies."

"They're kept in a locked box, with all the others," Phillips added.

"This place is clearly a bachelor pad, but it's high end, and not unusually messy," Ryan continued, wandering back through to the main, open plan living space. The layout was very similar to the flat he'd once owned, if slightly smaller, and he found that his feet knew where to take him even before his mind instructed them to walk.

"There's another computer here," Phillips called out, from the spare bedroom, which Harding had evidently used as an office. "Password protected, as usual, so we'll add this to the list for Digital Forensics to have a look at."

They'd taken the precaution of wearing nitrile gloves and shoe coverings, so Ryan lifted a few papers strewn on the desk, only to find they were invoices from past jobs. His eye fell on a stray USB cable attached to the computer, and wondered if that was where Harding used to charge his phone.

Except, the connector didn't match the model of iPhone Harding had favoured.

"Any storage devices around here?" he murmured.

They looked around the desk and inside the drawers, but found none.

"There weren't any external storage drives found in his car, either, were there?" Ryan said, and Phillips shook his head.

"Nothing on the inventory," he said. "Why?"

"He's a photographer," Ryan said. "The file sizes will be enormous; he couldn't manage with the storage provided on a regular hard drive, not if he was taking hundreds of high-resolution images at a time. He would have needed at least one heavy-duty external storage drive."

"What about cloud storage?" Phillips wondered.

"Some people love it, some people hate it."

Ryan slipped onto the desk chair, trying to imagine Harding at work there, and where he might have kept things. Swivelling round, he found himself looking at a wall of bookshelves filled with books that, from the dusty look of them, were mostly there for show—or, perhaps, to impress his latest conquest.

All dusty, except one small patch on one of the upper shelves.

Coming to his feet again, Ryan crossed the room and stood in front of the shelves, frowning at the patch which looked as though it had been freshly cleaned, and then lifted his hand to feel around the top of the books.

"*Bingo*," he said. There, in his hand, he held an external USB drive.

"You must have a sixth sense," Phillips declared. "Although, it's probably encrypted."

"We'll send this off to forensics, and see what they can do," Ryan said, and tapped the heavy chunk of plastic against his hand.

Half an hour later, they left the apartment, locking it safely behind them and sealing the door with police tape until Faulkner's team could come and sweep through every inch of the place.

As they made their way back down to the ground floor, Ryan gave a funny little laugh.

"What is it?" Phillips asked him.

"I just realised, I didn't think about Edwards or my sister at all, the entire time we were in there," he said. "D'you think this means I've laid their ghosts to rest?"

"You? Don't be daft," Phillips scoffed. "You've just found a new one to worry about, that's all."

Which was, of course, perfectly true.

CHAPTER 13

Will Harding had not, it seemed, been the beneficiary of a family that was independently wealthy, nor anywhere close to it. However, he had been loved; a fact that was painfully obvious to Ryan and Phillips as they seated themselves in the small living room of his parents' home, and forced themselves to face the ravages of another family's grief.

"Once again, we are very sorry for your loss," Ryan said quietly, as Laura Harding wept silently on the sofa.

The words were trite but sincere.

"I—I just—I can't understand what happened—"

His mother struggled to speak, and her husband moved closer, wading through his own stony-faced grief to put an arm around her shoulders.

"Howay, lass," he said softly. "There, now."

Her chest heaved and fell, and her eyes, when she looked up again, were horribly swollen inside a face that was as pale as the magnolia walls at her back.

"Nobody is giving me any answers," she muttered, suddenly angry with all of them. "Nobody! I'm being fobbed off by a bunch of idiots calling themselves Family Liaison Officers—"

"They're just doin' their jobs," Stephen argued, although he barely had the energy. "They're not to blame."

"Who *is*?" she almost shouted. "Do *you* know? Do *you*?"

She turned on Ryan and Phillips, who met her anger with a patience borne of long experience. There was a cycle to grief, as they both knew themselves, and that cycle needed to run its course through to acceptance.

"We don't know what exactly happened yet, Mrs Harding, but we're working very hard to find out," Ryan told her, and something in his voice must have been reassuring, because her body seemed to visibly relax. "At first, the circumstances of your son's death appeared to be accidental, but I'm afraid we don't believe that to be the case, anymore. We're actively investigating his death as suspicious—"

"What…what does that mean, exactly?" Stephen said.

"It means we are investigating all possible causes of death, including murder or manslaughter."

"I'm sorry, but we've never had any dealings with the law, or the police," she mumbled. "I don't know what happens next…what do we do?"

She looked up and into his eyes, and Ryan felt a part of his heart shatter for the woman who had birthed a happy, dark-haired little boy once, whom she would never see again.

"You don't need to do anything, except take care of each other," he said, once he was able. "We'll be doing all the work behind the scenes to find those responsible for Will's death. If you feel able to help us by answering a few questions—"

"Yes," she said, eagerly. "Yes, of course we will, won't we, Steve?"

She nudged her husband, whose mind was only half present, the other half being far away in the sands of time as he remembered playing football on the beach with his son, years before.

Go on, lad! Curl it around, that's the way!

"—Steve?"

He nodded, wearily. Whatever you need."

"Thank you," Ryan murmured, and, to his relief, saw that Phillips was already typing a message on his smartphone to the Family Liaison, instructing them to make the arrangements for an expedited course of grief counselling sessions.

"The first thing I need to ask is a bit of a personal question about Will's circumstances," he began, and watched surprise register briefly on their faces.

"His circumstances?" Laura repeated. "What d' you mean?"

"I mean, things like his source of income," Ryan explained. "Did your son make money any other way, aside from his photography work?"

They looked at each other, then shook their heads. "No, not that we know of," his mother replied. "Why is that important?"

"Just standard questions," Ryan smiled, and moved swiftly onto the next. "What about his friends? Did he have a circle of longstanding friends, or had he made any new ones, lately?"

"Will had two very good friends from school, Mark and Ash—Ashok, that is. I can give you their details if you'd like, although Mark lives in Canada now, and Ash is in London, so I don't know if they'd be able to tell you much about what's been happening up here."

"You never know," Phillips said. "If Will kept in touch with them, he might have mentioned something on the phone."

"And anyone new in his life?" Ryan prodded, once they'd handed over the contact details for Will's old school friends.

"Well, there always seemed to be some new girl or another," his mother said. "I kept hoping he'd find someone special and settle down, but he was enjoying himself too much."

"Always had a way with the lasses," his father said, with a touch of pride, before his face crumpled again.

"*Steve*," his wife sobbed, and took his hand between both of her own.

Ryan and Phillips waited, giving them time to pause and recover themselves, which was the right thing to do but also happened to be the most effective way to handle an emotional witness. It was short-sighted to push too hard, until they were so broken they could remember and tell you no more; it was far better to tread slowly, carefully, and with compassion.

"I can't remember Will mentioning any new friends in particular," his mother said, after a few minutes ticked by. "I messaged him on Friday and he told me he was fine, and he was going fishing for a couple of hours before he was due to photograph a big retirement party. He said it was a boring commission, but it paid well."

Ryan's ears sharpened.

"Fishing?" he repeated. "Was he a regular angler, then?"

"He mentioned it quite a bit," his father said. "He told us he'd won prizes for his catches, and he often took us out for nice meals to celebrate."

Ryan smiled, but knew that something didn't add up. For one thing, there'd been no evidence of any fishing equipment, books on fishing or clothing in Harding's flat or in his car, which was surprising if the man was becoming a serious enthusiast. For another, the picture they were developing of Will Harding was of a man who liked nice things, especially if they were expensive or labelled. He liked pretty women on his arm, preferably several, so long as none of them found out about each other, and he had a certain degree of vanity that was evident in his taste in clothing and homewares, amongst other things. Frames on the walls of his apartment showed glossy, black and white stills of local landscapes or fashion models; they didn't feature the happy face of a man stepping down as Men's Team Captain at a regional golf club.

It seemed like the wrong setting for a man like Will Harding, and the only explanation Ryan could conjure was the idea that Harding had run low on funds, and had therefore been forced to accept a commission that would meet any bills that were mounting up. If he was living beyond his means, it was likewise possible he might have borrowed money from the wrong places, and they'd called in the debt.

They needed to know his transactional history, and whether any communications had been deleted.

"Was there anything else?" Stephen asked, but it was clear they'd both hit a wall.

"Not for today," Ryan said. "Please, try to look after yourselves, and we'll be in touch as soon as we have any updated news."

"When will that be?" his mother cried.

"I don't know, Mrs Harding, but I'll be calling you, either way."

"Thank you," she murmured.

"We'll see ourselves out," Phillips said, and left them to their memories.

Outside, they walked the short distance to Ryan's car, which was parked a few doors along at the side of the kerb in the cul-de-sac where Harding had played on his first bike, and broken his ankle while trying to flip a skateboard.

"What do you make of that?" Ryan asked, once they were inside.

"The fishing was a red flag for me," Phillips said, "He's the last person I'd imagine sitting quietly beside a river or a lake, passing the time while he waited for something to bite."

"I agree, it doesn't seem to fit his character," Ryan said. "Which is why I wondered whether the 'fishing' was a metaphor for something different."

"Like what?"

"Well, what else could symbolise fishing or having a fish on a line?" Ryan wondered aloud. "It screams 'benefactor' to me, or someone he likes to think of as a sponsor."

"It's a definite angle," Phillips said.

"Your puns are getting worse," Ryan grumbled, as he started the car. "But I hope you're right, because, if the finances are a dead end, personal relationships are a dead end, along with all the usual motivations somebody might have to kill another person, and there's no suspect DNA, then I don't know where else we start to look."

He sighed, thinking of what they knew so far.

"We've got a body that we're almost certain has been moved," he said. "We've got five golf buggies, all freshly jet-washed by the usual mobile cleaning company nobody remembered to cancel, and we don't know whether that has destroyed trace evidence of a body having been transported in the back of one of them, but it's the best explanation so far. Aside from that... we've got *nowt*, as you would say."

"Ah, something'll turn up," Phillips said, with his trademark optimism. "It always does."

"Let's hope so, because, if it doesn't, I don't know how we'll be able to face his mother."

On which sobering thought, they left, each man ready to return to the comfort of home, and to be reminded of all that was good in the world.

CHAPTER 14

"Alan! For God's sake, man, get down!"

The landlord of *The Feathered Nest* was a generous soul, but his generosity was not without limits, much like alcohol consumption, and one look at the ruddy, bleary-eyed face of his longstanding regular, and sometime friend, Alan Hopkins, was enough to tell him that the man was several drinks past his personal limit.

"Alan, I mean it, I want you down off that table before you do yourself an injury."

"*Awww*, howay, Eddie," came the slurred reply. "I'm jus—just havin' a laugh—" Alan burped loudly, and a nearby table of punters looked on with disgust.

If it had been anyone else making a nuisance of themselves, and putting off other paying customers, Eddie would have ejected them from his family-friendly establishment without a second thought. But he'd known Alan a long time, and had good reason to allow him a bit more rope than most. He remembered, all those years ago, that it had been Alan who'd encouraged others to start coming along to *The Feathered Nest*, when he'd first bought the ailing pub and poured his life savings into bringing it back to life. Alan had been a real friend to him, back then, when his farm was doing well, and he'd been a happy man with a happy family.

Now…

Life moved on, Eddie thought, with sadness. Times were tough for farmers, especially those on the brink of losing all they'd worked for. Unable to beg, borrow or steal any more, Alan had turned to the only thing he had left…

Drink.

He felt sorry for Kath, his wife, who'd stuck by him through the years—but her generosity had its limits, too.

"Right, Alan, time for you to go home."

"He's alreet, Ed, leave'm alone, eh?"

This, from Alan's so-called 'friend', a man by the name of Tom Marshall, who laboured for Alan around the farm and seemed to spend much of his time pressing more alcohol into the older man's hand.

"You, shut your mouth, or you'll be out on your ear," Eddie told him, and pointed towards the door. "You're lucky I haven't barred you both."

Perhaps he should have done, he thought, but knew he couldn't bring himself to turn his old friend out into the cold.

He was about to go and call for a taxi, when there came the sound of an enormous crash, followed by the shocked cries of several nearby tables. Eddie hurried back around the bar to find Alan lying spreadeagled on the floor, blood dripping from a wound at his head but, thankfully, still conscious.

"Alan!"

He rushed across, whipping out a bar towel to stem the flow of bleeding. "You daft bugger," he muttered, and turned to find Tom swaying nearby. "Come and hold this towel against the wound, while I ring for an ambulance."

Tom yawned, but did as he was told.

Twenty minutes later, an ambulance arrived, which was the fastest any medical vehicle could have driven along the narrow country lanes to their remote spot. He watched Alan and Tom clamber into the back of the van, Alan already wailing about the state of the country and how politicians had no respect for people who were the salt of the earth, like him, while Tom sang a loud, off-key version of 'Roxanne'.

Eddie stepped back inside his pub, made the usual apologies to his other customers, and then walked back to the staff telephone where he keyed in a number he knew by heart.

After a few rings, it answered. "Hello?"

"Kath? It's Eddie," he said.

There came an audible sigh down the line. "What's he done, this time?"

"Hurt his head," he replied. "I've sent him off to A&E with Tommy Marshall, if you want to go and see him."

Kath closed her eyes, but did not cry.

Not this time.

"For years, I've gone down to the hospital and faced the pitying stares from the doctors and nurses," she said. "I've tried to ignore it, and tell myself he's not well, but, Eddie, I just can't do it anymore. I've had enough of it, and of him—"

"Kath—" he protested.

"*No*," she said, vehemently. "I deserve to be happy, Ed. I used to love him, so much...*so much*. But watching him these past few years, hearing him rant and rave and hate the world, I can hardly remember the man I fell in love with. As for the drink..."

Eddie ran a hand over the back of his neck, feeling terrible for any part he'd played in that. "I should have recognised that he had a problem, sooner than I did," he admitted. "I'm sorry for that, Kath, really I am."

"He's responsible for his choices," she said, not willing to give any quarter. "Believe me, I've made all the excuses under the sun, but I'm done with that, now. Let Tommy hold his hand; he seems to prefer the company of that layabout, anyhow."

"I'm sure that's not true," he said.

"Isn't it? Tell that to my husband."

With that, the line went dead, and Eddie slowly replaced the receiver. Back in the cold interior of their farmhouse, where the electric had been cut off for the second time in as many months, Kath shivered, not noticing the tears rolling slowly down her face.

As she dragged herself up the stairs towards the master bedroom they no longer shared, Kath stopped to look at an old frame featuring a young couple standing in front of a church, showered in confetti. The woman looked happy and carefree, her face upturned and smiling, while the young man standing beside her looked handsome and vital, the very picture of health.

"Goodnight, Alan," she whispered, and carried on up the stairs.

CHAPTER 15

The next day

Kath Hopkins awoke to a cold, silent house.

There came no comforting snore from across the hallway, and she surmised that Alan had slept elsewhere, most likely in their local hospital or down at the police station, depending on his behaviour. In years gone by, she'd never have left him alone, but she had nothing left in her to give. Besides, Tom was with Alan, and, with the pair of them gone, who else would give the animals their morning feed?

Tired, so tired of it all, she dragged her weary body from the bed and hurried to the bathroom, braving a cold shower now that the electric was off before hurrying into several layers of clothing to try to insulate herself. She'd have liked a cup of tea, but, since that wasn't possible, she settled for a cup of water, which she drank in the sitting room, staring sightlessly at the wall of framed pictures she'd once put up, so lovingly. They featured years of memories, of she and Alan at county shows and of the children at their gymkhanas, but, as the kids had grown and left the nest, life had changed for the worse. The boys hadn't wanted to take over the running of the farm and, unlike Alan, she couldn't really blame them. It wasn't a life for everyone, and they had their own dreams to pursue.

She smiled a little as she thought of Danny, who was living in Edinburgh and running his own artisan coffee shop. Alan hadn't understood, the first and only time he'd visited his son's new business. He hadn't understood why anyone would want to grow a beard and stand behind a counter, serving fancy coffees, when he could be master of acres of land, and a part of the basic cycle that kept their country running and its people fed. Danny had tried to explain it to him, and spoken of the growing turnover, hoping for a word of encouragement from the father he'd idolised since birth.

But none had been forthcoming.

Looking back, that's when she'd started to love him a little less than before, Kath realised. The man she'd married would never have belittled his own child, nor let the vagaries of a changing economy change his fundamental character. So what, if they had to make changes, or try something new? The Alan she'd known would have sighed a little, but then found the positive in a bad situation. He'd have shaken himself off, and reached for new stars, grateful to have a loving family around him who would support him all the way.

But Alan hadn't done that.

Oh, no.

Kath drained the cup of water she held, and then rose to pad back through to the kitchen, remembering the first time he'd shoved her against that wall, over there—or thrown her favourite china teapot against the other wall, over there.

Slowly, over time, every happy memory their house had ever held had been replaced by bad ones, and Alan became that which he'd always hated: a tyrant, a bigot, an angry, embittered man without a good word to say about anyone.

As for the drinking...

She shook her head, and leaned against the edge of the sink.

Then, after her body shook silently for a few minutes, she sucked in a deep breath and forced herself to continue the day, and to face whatever mood Alan would be in, when he finally came home.

"Time to feed the animals," she said to the empty room.

A few minutes later, Kath pulled on an ancient pair of muddied wellies she kept on a stand just outside the front porch, zipped up her coat, and stepped outside into the drizzly morning. Yesterday, the sky had been awash with sunshine, but today the hills of Northumberland swam with heavy fog that clung to the hedgerows. On another day, she might have thought it a pretty sight, but not that day. She peered out into the gloomy morning with trepidation, feeling the crushing loneliness of one who had no other person for company, either in body or in mind.

At least, not until later.

Kath shook herself, and stepped out into the misty morning, her booted feet squelching against the muddy courtyard. She spent half an hour systematically feeding the animals, before remembering she needed to hop across to the far field and top up the cows' trough of feed over there. It was always her least favourite job, because it involved walking all the way down to the road which ran through their farmland, and across to the cow shed on the other side. It was a fair distance in rainy weather, especially since the quad bike hadn't had a lick of petrol in it for weeks.

Duty overcame any feelings of tiredness, and she made the slow journey down the lane towards the road, which split the land in two. She looked both ways through the fog and was about to step onto the tarmac when she spotted the headlights of a car approaching at speed. It wasn't unusual for drivers to drive fast in those parts, because many of the locals who used the road were so used to the terrain it had become second nature to them, so she wasn't especially worried and simply stepped back onto the grass again to wait for the car to pass.

But it didn't pass.

To her horror, she watched the car change direction at the last moment and veer towards her, very deliberately. There was no time to run, no time to react before its bumper hit her body with a sickening crunch and sent it flying through the air, where it landed in the sodden earth, broken and bleeding.

Miraculously, Kath regained consciousness, and her first thought was that she was already dead. The pain in her body was indescribable, and she could barely breathe through the crushing weight of two broken ribs and a collapsed lung. Both of her legs were broken and twisted beneath her at unnatural angles. Her head throbbed with the pain of impact against the rough earth, but it was her midsection that suffered the most, and, through the haze of fear and trauma, she knew that, unless someone were to find her and take her to safety soon, she would certainly die out there, alone.

Through the sound of her own laboured breathing, she heard the tread of footsteps approaching, and, for a moment, felt relief that someone had stopped to help. Or perhaps it hadn't been a hit and run, after all, but a driver who'd lost control of their vehicle and was now hurrying to help his victim.

It was neither of those things, as she soon came to learn.

Hard hands grasped the neck of her coat and dragged her towards the centre of the road, uncaring of the pain or the fact she should not be moved. Kath tried to find the words to beg them to stop, but her mouth pooled with blood and the world was already turning dark again. She heard the rasp of her clothing against the tarmac, tried to see the outline of their face but could see only endless grey sky until the rasping stopped and their face suddenly appeared above her.

Kath's vision wavered but, as she caught sight of the person who was responsible, her last thought was one of confusion and terror. There was no conversation, no pity nor delay. They took a fistful of her hair, lifted her head up like a rag doll, then sent her skull crashing back against the hard tarmac; once, twice, and a third time for good measure until her body no longer twitched and shook, but lay still.

Then they straightened, cast a furtive look around, and hurried back to their car.

Moments later, its tail-lights disappeared into the fog.

CHAPTER 16

Ryan's feet pounded the main road leading through Elsdon village, legs pumping as he covered the ground on the circular route he ran most mornings. He was about to tackle the steep incline leading to their home at the top of the hill when the music playing through his headphones gave way to an incoming call.

"Ryan," he said, and slowed to a walk.

It was the Control Room, with details of a new dispatch.

"I'll be there in"—he paused to consider the distances—"should be around forty-five minutes to an hour. Better send a local team to secure the area, and I'll be there as soon as I can."

After ringing off, he put a call through to Phillips, who answered immediately.

"Were you sitting on your phone or something?"

"Aye, I keep it in the crook of my arse at all times," Phillips shot back. "What's up?"

"I've just had a call from Control. There's been a hit and run fatality near Chollerford, not far from—"

"Heavenfield," Phillips said, remembering a time years before, when Ryan had found himself embroiled in a mystery at the isolated little church just outside the village of Chollerford, near Hadrian's Wall. "I can be there in half an hour."

"Good," Ryan said. "I'll tell Lowerson and Reed to keep progressing the investigation at the coast while we're dealing with this fresh one."

"What are the circumstances?"

"Bad," Ryan replied, succinctly. "A local woman was hit and seriously injured, then abandoned on the road. Nobody called for help until another local happened to drive by, but she was already gone by then."

"Poor lass," Phillips said, and made a note of the address.

Once he'd ended the call, Ryan pocketed his phone and stared at the hill stretching out before him. Then he pushed off at speed, sprinting upward as if death itself was snapping at his heels, arms and legs working until he reached the summit, where his girls waited for him.

He made his way indoors, never more conscious that the life they'd made rested upon the edge of a knife, as it did for everyone. Whether by accident or design, life could be snatched away in the blink of an eye, so it was better to live it to the full.

He cocked an ear, listening for the sound of morning cartoons or the slop of porridge hitting the floor that would indicate Emma was already up and rampaging about, but there was nothing except the distant sound of Anna running a shower in their ensuite bathroom.

Coincidentally, he needed a shower, too.

With a gleam in his eye, he summoned his remaining energy and took the stairs two at a time.

By the time Ryan's car pulled over onto the grassy verge near Hopkins Farm, he found Phillips already waiting for him with a lukewarm coffee.

"You're a good man," he declared, and took a deep, fortifying gulp.

Phillips watched him chug back the liquid. "Thirsty, eh?"

Ryan eyed him over the rim of the cup. "Yes," he said. "So?"

Phillips smiled. "Your workout a bit hard this mornin', was it?"

Ryan polished off the last of the coffee. "No harder than usual," he replied, keeping a straight face. "I like to keep up with my workouts, as you know."

"Best way, lad, best way. You don't want to start slackin' in that department, if you know what I mean."

Ryan snorted. "Frank, a blind, deaf mute from a non-English speaking country would still understand what you meant."

Phillips grinned, and then looked around. "It's a pretty spot," he remarked. "Even now, with the place shrouded in mist, it's atmospheric. On a clear day, I bet you can see for miles around."

"There's a song in there, somewhere," Ryan muttered, and they made their way across to where a couple of local bobbies stood guard behind the police line, which closed the road to the driving public while evidence was being gathered.

They spent a while talking with the first responders, who, Ryan was pleased to say, appeared to be competent at their jobs. They gave him a summary of the facts and of the victim, who was fifty-nine-year-old Katherine Hopkins, the wife of Alan Hopkins, the owner of nearby Hopkins Farm.

"Hang about, I recognise that name," Phillips said. "I'm sure Hopkins used to supply milk to schools. I remember seein' their milk bottles everywhere."

Hopkins Farm Milk.

"Must've been before my time in the North," Ryan said.

"I don't think they have the same sort of presence they once did," Phillips said. "I haven't seen their vans around much, or their cartons on supermarket shelves. Maybe the farmer retired."

"We can find out when we speak to him," Ryan said. "First, let's pay our respects to the dead."

For once, Phillips made no complaint, and the two men scribbled their names in the logbook, dipped beneath the police line and crossed the tarmac to where a pop-up forensics tent had been erected around Kath's body, to protect it from the elements and preserve any evidence that might be found.

"Knock, knock," Phillips called out, before entering.

Inside, they found Tom Faulkner and another member of his team crouched beside Kath's body, no part of their own bodies visible to the naked eye, having covered themselves completely from head-to-toe in clinical grade overalls, gloves, hairnet and hood, face mask and goggles.

Faulkner looked up, and held out a hand to indicate they should wait beside the doorway rather than step any closer to the body.

"Just a sec," he said, and snapped another close-up picture of the woman's face.

Ryan watched him work with speed and precision, and then made his own assessment of the scene. One thing that was abundantly clear from the outset was that Kath Hopkins must have suffered terrible pain before she died. The injuries to her head and limbs were visible and shocking, but they merely hinted at the dreadful internal damage that had probably caused her to drown in her own blood.

It was a horrible way to die, and Ryan's face became shuttered as he thought of the kind of sociopathic mind that could inflict terminal injuries such as these and then simply drive away. There was a callousness to it; a selfishness that was somehow worse to him than the many unprovoked attacks that might result in unplanned deaths, or the 'loss of control' moments that happened every day of the week. The act of abandoning a victim was a very deliberate one, and spoke to a particular type of mindset.

"Right." Faulkner stepped carefully around the body. "Another body, another tent."

"Very different circumstances, it seems?"

"Yes, quite different to our man up at Dunstanburgh," Faulkner replied. "Here, it's looks as though Mrs Hopkins was crossing the road to feed the cows on the other side, when she was run down. The impact was acutely traumatic, as you can see from her injuries."

"So you reckon it was a straightforward hit and run?" Phillips asked him. "Maybe the driver didn't see her through the fog until it was too late?"

"It's possible," Faulkner replied. "However, I have a few concerns."

They waited.

"In the first place, I'd suggest you draw Pinter's attention to the wound at the back of her head," he said. "It may be that the impact sent her flying backwards onto the tarmac, and she hit her head with sufficient force to split open her skull."

"But you don't think so?" Ryan guessed.

"No," Faulkner said. "It looks to me as if she's had at least three separate impacts to the back of her head, each at a slightly different angle, which you wouldn't find if she'd suffered a single blow following impact."

Ryan nodded. "Anything else?"

"Yes," Faulkner said, thoughtfully. "You see her legs? They're completely shattered, broken in numerous places, and yet they're laid out neatly side by side, as though they'd been arranged that way. In my experience with RTA's, victims never end up looking so neat."

There was that word again, Ryan thought.

Neat.

"The next thing to notice is the lack of any signs of harsh braking," Faulkner continued. "In cases of hit and run, you'd expect to see a driver slam on the brakes, and burn up the rubber on their tyres, but there's nothing like that to see on the tarmac, here." Faulkner pointed out a couple of faint track marks on the ground a few feet to their right, and they followed his line of sight. "The only thing you can see are these track marks, which look very fresh to me," he said. "They lead from the verge, over there, all the way to where the body was found, here, if you want to pop outside and have a look for yourself."

They took his advice, and followed the tracks, which had already been photographed. As Faulkner said, they led all the way to the verge, where they found another member of his team cataloguing the ground beside two deep parallel tyre marks.

"Looks to me like a car swerved off the road, then reversed back on again," Phillips said, after he'd studied the angles and direction of the tracks.

Ryan agreed. "It looks to me like this was the real impact site, and whoever was behind the wheel dragged Kath's body back into the middle of the road."

Phillips started to ask, 'why?', before the answer came to him. "It was deliberate, then?"

Ryan gave a brief nod, while his eyes continued to track the ground, committing it all to memory.

"If Kath was standing off the road, there's very little chance it could have been an accidental hit and run," he said. "The perp had to turn the car off the road to hit her, which demonstrates the requisite *mens rea*."

"D' you think it could be one of those cases where they lost control?" Phillips asked.

"To use that as an excuse, it would have to be a serious medical incident at the wheel, such as a heart attack," Ryan said. "And there's no way the driver could have suffered anything of the kind, if he or she was then able to drag Kath's body to the centre of the road, finish off the job with a few hard cracks to the back of her skull, and then drive away, happy as Larry."

He turned away, and looked out across the barren fields towards the stone farmhouse tucked behind a small cluster of trees, half a mile away. "This is a murder investigation now," he said simply. "I want a full history of the victim, Frank, but first, let's go and see whether her husband has a motive."

"Lead on, MacDuff."

CHAPTER 17

Meanwhile, in the village of Craster, Lowerson and Reed found themselves lost in translation.

"I told him to pick a chicken stick, but would he listen? Sure enough, the feller makes a chunk shot, then the ball went off like bloody airmail, straight down the carpet and off into the cabbage."

They stared at the former Men's Team Captain, Kevin Kincade, and tried to decipher what he'd just said.

"The ball...went into a bunker?" Charlie guessed.

"No, it never went into the cat box, but he was stuck in the rough for a full fifteen minutes, I can tell you." Kevin sniffed, authoritatively. "Anyway, I said to the missus, I've had enough of dealin' with these duffers," he carried on, pausing only to slurp noisily from a cup of tea. "If they don't want to listen to a more experienced player, that's their problem, I suppose. But golf isn't about lookin' good in pastels; you've gotta to know how to swing a banana ball and turn it into an albatross."

They stared at him, again.

"Yes, I can appreciate that," Jack said, and tried to drag the conversation back on track. "Tell us about the night of your retirement party, Mr Kincade. We're particularly interested to know whether you remember seeing or speaking to the photographer, Will Harding."

Kevin set his cup down and pointed a finger. "*There* was another poser," he said, not choosing to mince his words. "Flittin' around the room chattin' up all the women—my wife included—givin' them all the bumf about them and their daughters being *sisters*…I never heard such a load of old balls."

The wife in question looked wistfully over his shoulder, remembering the thrill of it.

"We understood Mr Harding stayed mostly on the side lines of the event, taking pictures at a discreet distance?"

"You must be jokin'," Kevin said. "Every time I looked around, he was gabbin'." He used his hand to parody someone talking too much. "I'm surprised there were any pictures taken at all. He seemed to be gettin' somewhere with Molly," he added. "Those two would have made a good pair, mind you. Both thought they were the bees knees, and obviously had a taste for *things*."

"What do you mean, Mr Kincade?"

"You know, all that designer stuff," he said, and gave an eloquent shrug. "Labels on everything, and deep pockets, come to that. I tell you, I never knew photography was so lucrative."

Neither did they, Charlie thought, and stumbled along the same line of thought as Ryan had, the previous day, asking herself how Harding managed to fund such an extravagant lifestyle.

"Could've sworn he had an Omega on his wrist," Kevin tagged on, thereby demonstrating an admirable knowledge of 'things', himself.

"Do you remember the last time you saw Mr Harding on Friday evening?"

"I'd had a skinful by the end," he admitted, and his honesty was refreshing. "I'm not sure

I was in any fit state to know what time it was, or who was where. Brenda practically wheeled me home in a barrow—didn't you, love?"

His wife smiled weakly, and nodded.

"You can't recall seeing Mr Harding at any particular time, then?"

"Well, now I think of it, I'm sure I saw him talking to Molly sometime around ten o'clock," he said. "I saw them sneaking off down one of the corridors, not long afterwards."

They came to full alert.

"*Together?*" Jack queried. "Do you know where they went?"

"Well, son, I might be a bit long in the tooth but I'm not a complete dinosaur," he said. "We used to sneak off in my day too, you know."

"Of course, I—"

"Back then, we'd go behind the bus shelter, or down by the dunes—didn't we, love?"

His long-suffering wife nodded, and became wistful again.

"Not so, nowadays," he said to them. "I watched them, bold as brass they were. He went off, first, and closed himself off in the disabled toilet. Thirty seconds later, if that, I saw her scuttlin' off in the same direction. She came out again a few minutes later."

Charlie looked across at Jack, who nodded.

"That's very helpful," he said. "Do you remember seeing Mr Harding come out of the bathroom, too?"

"Well, I *assume* it was the bathroom," Kevin said. "There isn't much else down that corridor, except a few cupboards, which strike me as a bit poky, if you were aimin' for a hole in one—"

"*Kevin!*" his wife hissed.

"I'm only sayin'," he muttered. "Besides, come to think of it, I didn't see that photographer feller come back into the room, after then." Kevin became thoughtful, casting his mind back.

"No," he said quietly. "I didn't see him, after then."

A short while later, Lowerson and Reed made their excuses and left the Kincade household, before any further golfing anecdotes could be unleashed upon them.

By mutual accord, they walked down towards the harbour, breathing in the charcoal scent of freshly smoked kippers as they passed *Robson's*.

"What d' you make of Kevin's account of things?" Charlie asked, after a minute or two. "I can't see Molly Finch clubbing a man twice her size, hiding his body and then dragging it down to the thirteenth hole, sometime later in the night."

"Neither can I," Jack said, and began walking along the stone pier attached to the outer wall of the harbour, which afforded a picture-perfect view of Dunstanburgh Castle from beneath its arches. "What I can easily imagine is the two of them setting up a rendezvous somewhere down the service corridor, and Molly being too embarrassed or worried to tell us that part of her evening. It wouldn't be the first time a witness has edited their version of events."

Charlie nodded, thinking back to their interview the previous day. "Molly is also an opportunist, if I'm not mistaken," she said. "If she thought there was any possibility of a new catch, she'd be unlikely to want to discuss too many details about an old one, if you get my meaning."

He looked at her in total confusion. "Who's the new catch?"

Charlie gave him a lopsided smile. "Are you telling me you didn't realise she was flirting with you, yesterday?"

Jack's eyebrows flew into his hairline. "No, I mean...*no*, I just thought that was her general demeanour..."

He began to turn a slow shade of red, and, oddly, she found it endearing. The one thing that she and Kev Kincade could agree on was a mutual dislike of 'posers'; she'd had enough experience of those to last her a lifetime.

Then, Jack began to laugh. "You know, it's usually Ryan who has to deal with swooning women. I should enjoy the novelty, I suppose."

She wasn't hypocrite enough to argue; many people would be affected by the way their boss happened to look, but two things could be true at once. Jack Lowerson might not look like he'd walked off the set of *Superman*, but he wasn't half bad to look at, either. She knew many women who'd find his 'boy next door' demeanour quietly attractive...

Women like you? her mind whispered.

Taken aback by her own train of thought, Charlie moved a little further away from him, and they walked at a safe distance towards the far end of the pier.

"We could re-interview Molly, and give her the opportunity to amend her statement," he said. "Then, I guess we speak to Faulkner to see if his team have found any trace DNA in any of the toilets or cupboards down that utility corridor."

Charlie cleared her throat and nodded. "That corridor also leads down to the kitchen, and the back entrance to the clubhouse," she said. "They keep a bank of golf buggies directly outside that back entrance, as well."

"Easy access," he agreed.

They came to the end of the pier and dipped beneath a stone arch, where they looked north along the cliffs where Ryan and Phillips had walked, the day before. Dunstanburgh rose up from the rocks at the far end, dwarfing the villages that had sprung up at its feet.

"If only walls could talk," she said.

"Or golf buggies," he added, to make her laugh.

CHAPTER 18

The door to the Hopkins' farmhouse was opened by a tall, well-built man with a thatch of curly hair that had once been dark, but was now peppered with grey. He wore a clean, well-fitting blue shirt over jeans and boots, but his face was sombre, and it seemed obvious that he'd been weeping at some point during the course of the morning.

"Can I help you?"

"Mr Hopkins? DCI Ryan and DS Phillips, Northumbria CID—"

He held up a hand to interrupt them. "It's Alan you need to speak to," he said. "Come on through this way, he's in the living room. I'm Eddie Bell, I own *The Feathered Nest* at the bottom of the hill."

"Lovely pub," Phillips chimed in. "We've had some beautiful Sunday lunches in there."

"Glad to hear it."

They followed him through a cold, darkened hallway into a faded living room that was similarly unlit, aside from a fire that crackled in the grate of an open fireplace. A man of around Eddie's age, somewhere in his mid or late fifties, was slumped in an easy chair by the fire and looked very much the worse for wear.

"Alan? There's two gentlemen from Northumbria CID to see you about…it's about Kath."

Hopkins grunted and opened his eyes, which were bloodshot and swollen—though, whether that stemmed from inconsolable grief or a heavy night's drinking, they couldn't be sure. His face was unshaven and bruised, with a large bandage strapped around his forehead and another on his left wrist. His clothing was crumpled and stained, and carried a strong scent of stale alcohol and vomit, which made for a heady mix at eleven o'clock in the morning.

"She's gone," he said, wearily. "Kath's gone."

"We're very sorry for your loss, Mr Hopkins," Ryan said.

"Perhaps, I should leave," Eddie said quietly.

"No need for you to run off, Ed. They'll probably want to talk to you, next, so you can tell them all about how I made a fool of myself at the pub, last night."

"Alan—" Eddie made a token protest.

"What happened?" Hopkins asked them, suddenly. "Did she cross the road without looking? Is that it?"

"We're not entirely sure what happened, Mr Hopkins, but we're going to find out," Ryan replied, watching the shadows flit over the man's wasted face. "It would be very helpful if you felt able to talk to us about your wife's movements, yesterday and early this morning."

"That young woman—the policewoman—who came around earlier, said that Kath had been run over this mornin'," Alan said. "What does yesterday have to do with it?"

"We're trying to build up a picture in our minds of your wife, and of the hours immediately prior to her death," Ryan explained, choosing not to mention their current thinking around Kath Hopkins having been murdered.

Alan nodded and gestured towards the sofa. "Take a seat."

They took up his offer, while Eddie remained standing by the door.

"Let's start with what happened yesterday," Phillips said.

Alan rubbed the side of his temple. "It was the same as every other day," he said, bleakly. "I woke up a bit late, maybe nine or ten, and, by that time, Kath had already fed the animals. She was on at me again about the electric, and that I should just call the company to sort it out. They're sayin' I owe them this an' that, but I've got a ledger that shows just how much they've been overchargin' me, all these years. I told her, I not payin' them another penny until I get a rebate."

Phillips thought he heard a quiet sigh from the back of the room, where Eddie stood listening to the patter he'd heard countless times before.

"Look, I'm not goin' to pretend we had the perfect life, because we didn't," Alan said, belligerently. "It's hard graft, runnin' a farm, and harder still when you've got the tax man after you for money you just don't have. I told her, it's this blasted government lookin' to squeeze everythin' they can from the workin' man—"

"We appreciate your candour, Mr Hopkins," Ryan said quietly. "Focusing on your wife's movements, yesterday, can you tell us what she did after feeding the animals?"

Alan coughed, and took a long drink from a glass of water Eddie had left on the table beside him.

"She was here until about two o' clock, sittin' there, readin' her books, all about romance with some foreign sheik or Scottish laird or whatever the hell it was."

Ryan's eye flicked to a small bookcase beside the other easy chair in the room, where there was a stack of Mills and Boon romance novels, all well-thumbed. He thought of the placement of the chairs, one either side of the fireplace, and of the wall of framed pictures of the couple's children from years gone by, and found himself wondering where it had all gone wrong between them. At one time, surely Alan and Kath would have shared their day beside a cosy hearth, laughed together and shared their hopes and dreams, but it was hard to imagine.

"Did your wife go out at any time?"

"I couldn't say. I left her to it, and was out for most of the afternoon, proppin' up the bar, wasn't I, Eddie?"

The landlord didn't smile, for there was nothing to smile about. "Alan came into the pub at around half past two," he did say, and Phillips made a note. "He was with us for the whole afternoon and evening, along with Tom Marshall."

"Havin' a good time with friends, that's what I was doin'," Alan put in.

"Who's Tom Marshall?"

"Works for me, here at the farm," Alan said, and, from the corner of his eye, Phillips saw Eddie fold his arms in a gesture of frustration. "We're mates, now."

They took down the man's details, before moving on.

"We understand you were in hospital overnight," Ryan said. "Can you tell us what happened, please?"

Conscious that Eddie was listening to every word, Alan didn't bother to sugar coat it.

"Tommy and me drank the bar dry. We were havin' a bit of a sing-song—"

"Dancing on the table," Eddie put in, quietly. "Disrupting the other patrons."

"You've got no sense of humour, that's your trouble," Alan muttered. "So, I took a bit of a tumble and banged my head...it was nowt but a bruise, but the doctor seemed to think I needed to stay in for observation, so I slept it off in a hospital bed in Hexham."

Hexham was an historic market town a few miles yonder, which had a well-equipped hospital serving that part of the county.

"Alan, you were concussed," Eddie said, and turned to Ryan and Phillips. "I sent him off in an ambulance with Tommy, but I got a call from one of the nurses later on to say that Tommy had taken himself off home, apparently, and left Alan on his own. They asked if I'd go down the following morning to pick him up."

Ryan turned back to Alan. "Didn't your wife visit you in the hospital?"

"She had better things to do, didn't she, Eddie?"

The landlord heaved another sigh. "I rang Kath to let her know there'd been an accident, but she—ah—" He lifted a hand, and let it fall away again.

"She wasn't interested in seeing me," Alan muttered. "Just say it."

"She was *tired*," Eddie corrected him. "Of many things, Alan."

Unexpectedly, the man's lip began to wobble, and the lines on his skin crumpled like paper. "I can't turn back the clock," he whispered, and swiped a hand beneath his running nose. "I wish I could, but I can't—"

"Would you like a tissue, Mr Hopkins?"

He shook his head, and the action brought a fresh wave of aches and pains.

"Are you happy to continue?"

Alan looked across at the two men seated on the sofa and wondered what lay behind their professional smiles. The taller one was obviously the man in charge, which was unusual, since the shorter one was older and obviously experienced, which told him that the younger man wasn't to be underestimated…neither of them were.

"Ed came along and gave me a lift home, this morning," he said. "We saw the roadblock, but we didn't know it was because they'd found

Kath's body. One of the PCs came over to tell me the bad news, just after we got back here."

Eddie nodded. "That's about right," he said.

"You're obviously a friend of the family?" Ryan said. "How long have you known Alan and Kath?"

"Twenty years, at least," Eddie replied. "That's when I took over the pub."

"Oh, Eddie's a very close friend, aren't you, Ed?"

The landlord turned back to Alan and nodded, sadly.

"We were, once."

It took the best part of another hour to complete a preliminary statement and, by the time they were done, Ryan and Phillips were drained by the effort.

"I'm heading back to the pub soon," Eddie said, as he showed them to the door. "I want to make sure he's all right, but then I have to get back."

They nodded.

"You've been a good friend," Ryan said, and watched some unreadable emotion flit across the man's face, which might have been guilt. "Mr Hopkins mentioned his friend, Tommy. Do you know him well?"

"As well as I'd want to," Eddie told them, in an undertone. "He was taken on as a labourer for the farm, but I can't say he's ever done much labouring. He used to live-in, but Kath couldn't stand him and put up quite a fuss about it, so Alan kept him on with the proviso that he found his own place. That was seven years ago and, since then, they've been inseparable. They've got nothing in common, except a love of drink. I can't help wondering if Alan might have gone down a different path, if he'd never met Tommy."

Eddie looked out across the farmyard, with its rusted machinery and broken-down quad bike.

"I know what you're thinking," he muttered. "You're wondering why I let him come into the pub, when he's an alcoholic."

They knew the value of silence in drawing people out, and simply waited for him to say more.

"I know there's a duty of care, and I never forget that," he said. "I don't need to take money from them that should be at home, in their beds;

I do a good enough trade. But I've known Alan for a long time—long enough to know that, if he didn't come down to *The Feathered Nest*, he'd find another place that'd serve him, where he doesn't have friends who'd care enough to look out for him."

"And to let his wife know his whereabouts," Phillips put in.

Eddie nodded and then, gathering his courage, told them the other thing they had a right to know.

"I loved Kath," he said, and his voice broke. "I expect, over time, you might have found that out, so I'm savin' you the trouble. I loved her for years, but she never knew it. It was only when things became really bad between her and Alan that we started to become close." He glanced back inside the house, then away again. "Alan doesn't know," he said, keeping his voice down. "I don't want to add to his grief, but I don't want to keep anythin' from the police, either. Kath was lonely, and so was I. I'm not excusin' anythin', I'm just tellin' you how it was."

Ryan studied his face, and then nodded. "Thank you, Mr Bell. We appreciate your honesty. Hopefully, this won't need to become public knowledge, but I can never make any promises on that score."

Eddie nodded and turned to go back inside. "You said you were from 'CID'. Doesn't that mean you deal with murders?"

Ryan nodded. "Yes, Mr Bell. We believe Katherine Hopkins was murdered."

Eddie looked as though he'd taken a punch to the stomach.

"I—I don't understand," he said. "Nobody would have wanted to hurt Kath. Nobody."

"Somebody did," Phillips said. "Can you think of anyone, anyone at all, who might have held a grudge?"

Eddie shook his head, seeming to have aged in the space of just a few minutes.

"She led a quiet life," he said. "We were happy together, and we'd started to talk about ways she could leave him, as gently as she could." Eddie knuckled away tears. "She was a gentle person," he whispered. "Never hurt a soul in her life."

"Thank you for your help, Mr Bell," Ryan said, and, breaking his own rules, put a hand on the man's arm. "We'll do our best for her."

As they made their way back down the hill towards the road, Phillips looked across at his friend's profile, which was hard as granite.

"What d' you make of it all, then?"

Ryan's jaw clenched. "We've got a farm on its last legs, and a farmer with a drink problem, unable to pay his bills," he said. "They're living in cold, dark conditions, although that hasn't always been the case. If we look into his financials, I'm going to guess that we'd find him mortgaged to the hilt, crippled by debt but too far gone to work his way out of it. That's hard, on any level, but throw in a drinking problem and you've got the conditions for a really miserable home life."

"Aye, it can't have been much fun for her," Phillips said, thinking of the pictures he'd seen on the walls that showed a younger Kath, smiling with her husband. "You know I'm not one to condone cheatin', but…"

"Mitigating circumstances?" Ryan suggested.

"Aye, maybe. We're not the Morality Police, anyhow."

"No," Ryan said. "But deceit in one area of life can sometimes reveal a tendency towards deceit in other areas, which can be helpful to know."

"True enough."

"For instance, if Kath was able to have an affair with Eddie without her husband finding out about it, then it's possible she was secretive in other areas of her life," he said. "We need to look into the shadows, because, on the face of it, we've got a farmer's wife without any obvious enemies with a motive to kill her."

"Eddie isn't married, himself," Phillips thought aloud. "That rules out a jealous wife. Even if Alan did know about their relationship, he couldn't have done it, because he was in hospital under constant supervision the whole time."

"He could have asked his friend, Tommy."

"We'll check him out," Phillips said.

"I want to know if Kath had a life insurance policy," Ryan said. "There has to be a motive somewhere, Frank."

"We'll find it," the other man said. "We always do."

"There's something about this whole thing," Ryan muttered. "I can't put my finger on it, but—" He shook his head. "There've been a lot of accidental deaths, lately, and I'm starting to wonder if there isn't some connection."

"None of the cases are connected," Phillips said. "We've gone over it before."

Ryan looked back over his shoulder, at the farmhouse on the hill.

"Go over it again."

CHAPTER 19

The team reconvened at Police Headquarters at four o'clock, minus Frank, who'd excused himself since it was his turn to do the school run and—unbeknownst to his wife—he was looking forward to taking Samantha to the McDonald's drive-thru for their regular mid-week treat.

"Mac? You remember DC Charlie Reed?"

MacKenzie smiled, and held out a hand.

"Of course," she said. "Good to have you with us, Charlie."

Reed felt an immediate sense of kinship, and she understood then that being a part of Ryan's team was like stepping behind an invisible forcefield, and gave an immediate sense of safety to all who were within its fold.

"Thank you," she said. "I'm excited to work with you all."

"Right," Ryan said, and hitched a hip onto the desk at the front of the room. "Charlie? Why don't you kick things off, and tell us the status of the investigation in Dunstanburgh?"

She took a fortifying sip of coffee, and started from the top. "As you know, the body of twenty-eight-year-old Will Harding was discovered by members of Dunstanburgh Castle Golf Club early on Saturday," she said. "It turns out he'd been hired to photograph a retirement party the previous Friday evening, and the pathologist has estimated his time of death to be somewhere between ten o'clock that night, and two o'clock the following morning. Our interviews with key members of the club and attendees at the party have narrowed that to ten-forty-five on Friday night, because he was alive and well and captured on CCTV talking to Molly Finch at the bar, before then."

Charlie paused to collect her thoughts.

"This morning, Jack and I spoke with Kevin Kincade, whose retirement was being celebrated, and he told us that he witnessed Harding leave the bar area and go down the utility corridor at around that time," she said. "He also asserts that Molly Finch, who was working behind the bar, followed Harding down the corridor shortly afterwards, he assumes for an assignation in one of the rooms—there's a disabled toilet, the kitchen area, and two cupboards that are lockable. That corridor also gives access to the back door, so it's possible they might have gone outside, but there's no CCTV in that area so we're unable to verify that."

"What does Molly say?" Ryan asked.

"Her initial statement didn't mention any rendezvous with Harding," Charlie said. "In fact, she stated that Harding took her number then left."

"We paid her a second visit today, but she's adamant she didn't leave for any kind of private rendezvous," Jack put in. "She was quite angry at the insinuation."

Ryan had heard plenty of manufactured anger in his time. "Did you believe her?" he asked them both.

"Hard to say," Charlie said. "She was very believable."

"I agree," Jack said, and Ryan thought that Reed must have worked a miracle on her teammate, or else Jack had experienced an epiphany of some kind. "We checked the CCTV overlooking the bar again, and there are a few moments where Molly is out of sight. She could easily have been in the storage room, the loo, or just out of the field of vision on that ancient camera, so we can't draw many conclusions from that."

"The fact is, it's very unlikely Molly Finch could have bludgeoned Will Harding, hidden his body and then moved it later, without being seen," Charlie pointed out. "Especially as this would all be off the cuff, and she's a petite girl of nineteen. We can't find any evidence to suggest Harding knew anyone at the party or at the club before Friday night, including her, so it's hard to see what motive she would have had; if anything, she seems disappointed that he isn't around to do some free headshots for her."

"Any update on forensics?" Ryan asked.

Charlie nodded.

"Faulkner has confirmed in his preliminary report that there were no tracks around the body, and his team combed the beach but couldn't find any rock that might have been a murder weapon," she said. "It's possible, but unlikely, that any marks were washed away, or that the rocks shifted…but, as you've already pointed out, the placement of the body was above the water line."

Ryan nodded.

"His team have gone over the golf buggies, but they were jet-cleaned on Sunday morning; it's a standing appointment with a mobile cleaning company who do all sorts of vehicles, paving, guttering and all that. It was their regular slot to come and go over the buggies and nobody thought to cancel it."

"If we'd known about it, we would have," Ryan muttered. "Were they able to salvage anything useful?"

Charlie pulled a face, and shook her head.

"Not really. Faulkner says he's recovered multiple samples, but whether any of them match Harding, it's too early to say. He's sent them off for analysis, but there was no blood spatter or anything of that kind visible to the naked eye."

Ryan picked up a biro and began fiddling with it, as he thought about other avenues of enquiry.

"What about your interviews with the locals?" he asked. "Have they thrown up any potential suspects, or anyone with a motive, at least—or was the Club Secretary right about Harding not knowing anyone in the area?"

"Jack and I have spoken to as many people as we could, either in person or on the telephone," she said. "A few of them claimed to have seen Harding's pictures shared around photography groups online, but they'd never met him before the party on Friday night. He has no family in the area, nor any close friends living around that part of the coast, so it rings true that he'd be a stranger in those parts."

"So, we've got a large pool of potential suspects, but none of them seem to have anything that even remotely resembles a motive to kill Harding," he surmised.

"Pretty much," she said, apologetically. "To make matters worse, none of the partygoers went missing during the party for any significant period of time, and there's nothing to suggest the presence of an outsider coming in, either."

"Have we considered the possibility that Harding took a picture of something he wasn't meant to?" MacKenzie said, and all heads swivelled in her direction. "Married man with someone other than his wife, or vice versa?"

"It's a possibility," Jack said. "But Harding's camera was recovered, and, although it was smashed, Faulkner did find a memory card."

Ryan was intrigued.

"Anything interesting on it?" he asked.

"The card was intact," Jack told him. "Just pictures from the party, some landscapes, what looks to be a wedding…we need time to go through them all, but nothing that screams 'suspicious'."

"All the same, I'll authorise some extra testing from Digital Forensics," Ryan said. "If a photo has been deleted, possibly by Harding's killer, it would be a serious break in the case. It would also explain how young Will Harding managed to wine and dine his women in style, and could afford to live like a king."

"You're thinking blackmail?" Jack asked. "'It still comes back to the problem we've had all along. Harding didn't know anyone at the party, so there wasn't anybody to blackmail or anybody with motive enough to kill him in such an organised way."

"And yet, they did," Ryan pointed out. "There has to be someone with an axe to grind."

"We do know somebody with a connection to Will Harding," MacKenzie said, very casually.

"We do?" Charlie said. "Who?"

MacKenzie looked between the four of them.

"Marcus Atherton."

CHAPTER 20

"Who's Marcus Atherton?" Charlie searched her mental files but came up blank.

"Atherton was a longstanding journalist for *The Daily Chronicle*," Ryan said. "I had more time for him than most, because he respected the boundaries of privacy and believed in a code of ethics when it came to searching for his next scoop. People were always more important to him than a paycheck, which is a mark of integrity, in my book."

"There aren't many like that, anymore," MacKenzie agreed. "A dying breed."

"Sadly, that's the literal truth in this case," Ryan said. "Atherton was found dead in his home just before Christmas. The official cause of death was carbon monoxide poisoning but, yesterday, Pinter mentioned to me that Atherton's extended toxicology analysis had finally come back from the lab. Apparently, there was an undefined organic compound found in his blood, which sounds a lot like poison to me, but Pinter's speaking with colleagues who have more specialist knowledge, to try to identify what it is."

"I had Atherton's phone records analysed by the Cyber Terrorism Unit, who liaised with his phone provider," MacKenzie said. "I wanted to see if any records were missing from the phone's internal history, and indeed they were. It turns out Atherton made an outgoing call to a number shortly before he died, and that number belonged to our photographer friend, Will Harding. The call wasn't picked up, and Atherton didn't choose to leave a voicemail message, but he made it, nonetheless. The question is, *why*?"

Ryan turned to Charlie and Jack. "Is there any record of an incoming call to Harding's number?" he asked.

Jack made a grab for his laptop, and called up the spreadsheet sent through from their Digital Forensics team.

"What was the date and time?" he asked.

"It was around six weeks ago," MacKenzie said, and reeled off the specifics.

"Their search doesn't go back that far, but if we speak to Harding's phone provider, they'll be able to confirm it," he said.

"What's suspicious is that the call isn't listed on Atherton's phone, but it's on record at the phone company," Ryan said. "Did he make any other attempts to call Harding?"

MacKenzie shook her head. "It seems Atherton only made a single phone call to Harding, which wasn't picked up."

"If there was a professional relationship between them, perhaps where Atherton had commissioned Harding to take pictures to go alongside an article he was writing, or something like that, you'd expect his number to appear multiple times and for it to be saved as a contact in Atherton's phone. Since it doesn't appear, I think it seems obvious that the call history was doctored so it wouldn't appear in the list of past calls," Ryan said. "It seems strange to imagine Atherton doing this himself, before he died, so I think it's safe to assume this was done by a third party, possibly the person who killed him—"

"We still can't say for certain that he was killed," MacKenzie cautioned.

Ryan folded his arms. "Don't you think it's quite a coincidence that Atherton made a missed call to Harding, shortly before he died, and now Harding himself is dead? Both in circumstances we deem suspicious?"

"I know how you feel about coincidences," she said. "And, I have to admit, you haven't been wrong, so far…"

"You know why that is?" Ryan said, with the flash of a smile. "Because—"

"*There's no such thing as a coincidence*," Jack and MacKenzie chimed in, and Charlie laughed.

"Is this a mantra I should take note of?"

"No need," Jack said. "It's practically stamped on his forehead."

Ryan chose to ignore the impertinence, and hopped off the table to pace around a bit. "This is our first connection," he said. "We have to figure out what it means for both Atherton and Harding, separately and together. Mac? Why not re-interview Atherton's former editor at the paper and a few of his colleagues to see if they know of any relationship between the two men?"

"I'll keep the pressure on Pinter, too, for any update on that unidentified compound," she said.

"Good. Jack, Charlie? Finish up your work with the locals on your list and let me know if anything comes back from forensics and digital forensics. I want to know if any of Harding's electronics have been cleaned up, like Atherton's, or if any images have been deleted from his camera's memory card."

He paused, and flashed them a tigerish smile.

"We've caught a scent," he said. "Let's see where it takes us, shall we?"

As they packed away their papers and prepared to call it a day, Jack thought of the empty walls awaiting him at home and decided to prolong the moment.

"Anybody fancy a pint?" he asked.

"I would, but I've got to face the Chief," Ryan said, referring to Chief Constable Morrison.

"After that, I want to try and get home to catch Emma before bedtime."

"I would, as well, but I've got to go and pick Ben up," Charlie said. "He's at my mum's."

"Is Ben your partner?"

They all looked at Jack, who evidently hadn't realised that his new teammate was a mother.

"Oh," she said, with a touch of surprise. "Um, no, Ben is my little boy. My mother helps out with childcare, sometimes, although her condition is getting worse, so we'll have to make some adjustments soon. If I leave now, it'll be perfect timing to collect him."

In one crushing moment, it became obvious to Jack that he'd behaved like a Buffoon of the First Order. When he thought of his petulant sulk the previous morning, he could cheerfully have dug a hole for himself to have crawled into, for it was clear that Charlotte Reed was a hard-working person who asked no favours except common decency from others. She had responsibilities at work and at home that outweighed his own, by a long margin, and the prospect of moving to a new team based in Newcastle was obviously a great relief to her. Despite his frosty welcome, she'd persevered with him, made him laugh, and even *covered* for him in front of the others, extending a friendly olive branch though he hadn't deserved it.

In short, she was a better person than he.

"Don't forget to let me know when you need a hand moving your boxes," he said, and Charlie looked up in surprise. The idea of him helping her move house had been a private joke between them, but he was making the offer a real one, now.

"Thanks," she said, softly. "I'll let you know."

After the other two had left, Ryan hung back to speak with Jack.

"That was well done," he said quietly.

Lowerson shrugged. "I didn't do anything," he said. "I just thought she might need some help."

"We all do, sometimes," Ryan said, and put a brotherly hand on his shoulder. "I know you felt upset about having somebody new working with us, but I hope you know it doesn't mean we've forgotten Mel."

Jack nodded, and wondered if she would ever reply to his last e-mail. "I was so caught up in my own feelings, I couldn't see past the end of my nose," he said, honestly. "I'm sorry for that."

"No apology necessary," Ryan said. "And I think you've earned yourself a new friend, by the looks of things. Your offer meant a lot to her."

"Do you know if—ah—" Jack stopped himself asking a personal question.

"Whether she's married, divorced, widowed or otherwise?" Ryan put in for him, and watched Jack redden a bit. "Yes, I know, from her file. But I think we should wait for her to confide in us, if she chooses to."

Jack nodded, and looked around the room, at a loss. "I might put in a few more hours…see if I can get ahead on some of the admin," he said.

Ryan looked at the time, made a mental cost-benefit analysis of his options, and erred on the side of friendship.

"You know, I can probably manage a cheeky beer, after all," he said.

Jack brightened, instantly. "Are you sure? I thought Morrison threatened to skin you alive, last time you missed an appointment with her?"

Ryan made a sound like a raspberry. "I'll take my chances."

Phillips would never have thought he was the kind of police officer to dispose of material evidence but, when it came to the remains of two McDonald's 'Happy Meals', his morals flew merrily out of the window.

"Mum knows we do this every week, you know." His daughter polished off the last of her milkshake with a loud slurp, then added her cup to the recycling bin.

"You can't know for *sure*," he said.

Samantha looked at him with the kind of pity only a thirteen-year-old could convey; coincidentally, it was the same look she'd given him when he'd told her he had no idea who or what a 'Swiftie' was, "and it better not be slang for cigarettes".

"You're in denial," she said, and he couldn't entirely disagree with her. "Can we visit Pegasus this weekend?"

Phillips nodded, and slung an arm around Samantha's shoulders. "Course we can, love, if you'd like to?"

"I wish I could see him every day."

From any other child, it might have sounded spoilt; after all, how many children had horses at all, never mind ones they could visit and ride every day? However, this wasn't true of Samantha, who'd come to Frank and Denise in special circumstances, having had a unique childhood. Her own mother and father were both dead now, but, for a while, she'd been part of the travelling circus community owned and led by her biological father—who hadn't deserved the title. Her formal education had been patchy at best, and one of her only friends had been the horse she'd looked after with diligence and care since he'd been a foal, like herself. They were like siblings, and hated to be apart for long.

Phillips had thought of their special bond many times and wished he could think of a solution. The fact was, he was almost certain Ryan had already secured preferential rates for Pegasus' livery at the stables in Elsdon, which was just as well because, without it, there was no way that he and Denise could have afforded to keep the horse, no matter how much Samantha loved him.

As for being able to see him more often...

Even before Samantha had completed their little family, he and Denise had spoken often about moving further out from the city, perhaps somewhere by the sea—or inland, like Elsdon. But properties in Northumberland were in high demand, especially ones that came with a patch of land for a horse, in a nice area, so the cost was prohibitive and, despite keeping an eye on the house listings every couple of weeks, things weren't getting any more affordable.

"We'll have to make do with giving him lots of love and attention on Saturday and Sunday," he said. "Hey, you've got that event coming up soon, haven't you?"

They hopped back into his car and headed for home, with Samantha chatting happily about show jumping and how she'd love to be on the Olympic team, one day. Phillips could never have imagined a future in which he had a beautiful, intelligent little girl with a natural flair for horsemanship, but there it was. As he made all the right noises, and burst with pride as she told him of the maths test she'd recently aced at school, he reflected that life was a funny old thing.

You never knew what was going to happen next.

CHAPTER 21

The next morning

With the exception of Ryan, who was never late to the office except in circumstances of life or death, Jack Lowerson prided himself on being the first person to arrive at his desk in the mornings. He enjoyed having his pick of the parking spaces, he liked being the first to order from the Pie Van, and, despite being a vegetarian, occasionally to snaffle a sausage roll whilst nobody was any the wiser.

Everybody had their little secrets.

On this occasion, he was mortified to enter their open-plan office, sausage roll in one hand, coffee in the other, and find he was not the earliest bird to catch the worm.

"Morning, Jack!"

Charlie looked up from her new desk and smiled at him.

"You're an early riser," he blurted out.

"No choice, I'm afraid! Ben's always up with the larks," she said, cheerfully. "I left him watching cartoons with my mum, working on his second breakfast. I thought it would be a good idea to familiarise myself with the office, get myself set up on the system and all that."

He nodded, and surreptitiously polished off the last bite of his sausage roll.

"You—" He chewed and swallowed. "You want a coffee?"

"Already got one here," she said, and lifted a cup bearing the catchphrase, "BONNY LASS".

He slid into his own chair, diagonally across from hers on a bank of four, which meant that they could see one another through the gap between their desktop computers.

She caught his eye, and pulled a funny face.

Lowerson laughed, then his eye caught the framed picture of himself with Melanie.

His smile faded. "I was thinking I'd carry on with the list today," he said. "Get some admin done this morning, make a few calls, then head up to Embleton and have a word with some more of the partygoers."

"Sounds like a plan," she said. "Digital Forensics are still going over Harding's memory card, but they've already sent through some files they've recovered from the external hard drive found at Harding's flat."

"Oh, yeah?" Lowerson said. "Anything interesting?"

"Actually, I think there is," she said, and gestured for him to come around to look over her shoulder.

He didn't know why it should have made him nervous, but it did.

"These images were deleted, but you know most things can be recovered by some tech nerd or another," she said, and he found himself smiling again.

"Is that the job spec?" he asked. "Tech nerd?"

"If it isn't, then it should be," she grinned. "Anyway, look at these ones."

He peered over her shoulder at a series of grainy images showing a man in a very compromising position, kissing a young blonde woman against a wall in a dimly lit corridor.

"Ooh la-la," he said. "Maybe Mac was right about Harding having taken photos of things he shouldn't have. Do we know who either of these people are?"

"Wait and see," she said, and clicked a button to enlarge one of the images.

"Isn't that—?"

"Yup." She nodded, and leaned back so that her hair brushed against his face.

Jack stepped away, sharply.

"Sorry! Did I bump you?"

He swallowed. "No," he said, and pointed towards the screen again. "That looks very much like Fraser Duncan, our local Member of Parliament, wouldn't you say?"

"I'd say it's his spitting image," she replied. "I'm not sure who the blonde is, but it definitely isn't his wife."

"I think you've just found somebody with a motive to kill Will Harding."

"There's just one problem," she said.

"What's that?"

"He wasn't at the sodding party, was he?"

Jack swore, and sat down on the nearest desk chair, which happened to be the one right next to hers.

"Nothing's ever simple, is it?" he declared.

She looked across at his kind, open face, and then at the framed picture of the woman he wanted to marry.

"No, it isn't," she said quietly, and turned back to the screen.

Duncan Fraser, MP, lived in a large, double-fronted townhouse in a smart area of Newcastle known as Gosforth. It was expensive enough to befit his status, whilst being modest enough not to attract too much unwanted scrutiny of his expense account.

"Nice place," Phillips remarked. "A bit manicured, for my taste."

Ryan agreed; the home and front garden were both immaculate and well-designed, but there seemed to be no particular charm to it, despite everything being rigidly symmetrical.

Sometimes disorder and imperfection could be beautiful.

"Jack and Charlie reckon the bloke who lives here is the one in Harding's photos," Phillips continued. "Even if he is, it's a long leap to murder someone just because they caught you out."

"It depends on the character and mindset of the killer," Ryan replied. "In our collective experience, we've seen just about every variant, haven't we? The reasons people have for murdering others have ranged from the bizarre to the ridiculous, the psychopathic or insane and, occasionally, the mundane."

"Ain't that the truth," Phillips said. "Even if this feller's done for Harding because he managed to get a snap of him with his secretary, or whoever it was, I still can't figure out how he did it."

"I guess we'll have to ask him," Ryan said.

Unfortunately, when they knocked at the large, blue-painted front door, it was not Duncan Fraser who opened it, but his wife, Eleanor. Their first thought was that, although she was an attractive woman of fifty with a short, dark bob of well-dyed hair and a pretty, carefully tweaked face, she was most definitely *not* the blonde in the photograph.

"Thank goodness you've come!" she exclaimed, taking the wind completely out of their sails. "It's about time you turned up, but better late than never, I suppose."

They looked at her blankly.

"Mrs Fraser?" Ryan enquired, just to be sure.

"Yes, of course it's me," she said, irritably. "Aren't you going to come in and give me an update?"

They looked at one another, then back at her.

"I think there may have been some crossed wires, Mrs Fraser. I'm DCI Ryan, and this is DS Phillips, from Northumbria CID—"

"Well, at least they've sent someone with a bit of seniority," she interjected.

"Were you expecting one of our colleagues to attend your house?"

"Good *grief*," she said. "I rang the station over two hours ago, so naturally I've been sitting around here waiting for someone to turn up."

"What for?" Phillips asked, bluntly.

"This is turning into a farce," she said, becoming angrier by the second. "You know perfectly well why you were called out here; it's so you can tell me where our car is, of course!"

She looked at the pair of them as if they'd recently crawled out from beneath a rock.

"I think there's been a misunderstanding," Ryan said, and smiled winningly, while Phillips watched from the sidelines with a certain fascination. "We're terribly sorry to hear that you've been inconvenienced, Mrs Fraser."

She blinked and, being only human, was momentarily distracted from thoughts of missing cars by a man who looked like Paul Newman's better-looking brother and had a voice like smooth, clotted cream.

"Well...that's...that's all right," she said, and ran a hand over her hair.

"I believe you may be expecting some of our colleagues to attend regarding your stolen car," Ryan continued, while she continued to stare into his blue-grey eyes like a rabbit caught in the headlights. "We're here because we were hoping to speak with your husband regarding another matter—is he at home, at the moment?"

"No," she said. "Duncan's at his weekly surgery with his constituents. What do you need to speak to him about?"

Ryan didn't answer that but offered a diversion. "Well, while we're here, perhaps we could help by taking down some details about the stolen car. May we come in?"

She brightened up immediately. "Oh, that would be *wonderful*," she gushed, and stepped aside to allow them to enter the house. "Can I offer you a coffee, tea…perhaps a little slice of cake?"

Phillips closed the door behind them and watched his friend's retreating back with fatherly pride. "Aye," he said to himself. "The Force is strong with that one."

CHAPTER 22

The interior of the Fraser home was as bland and ordered its exterior, with acres of white walls and a permeating smell of something that was probably called 'Clean Linen' or 'White Cotton'. They happened to know the couple had lived there for eleven years, but there was no sign of the usual clutter and detritus they'd normally find in a working home. Here, there was a place for everything, and everything was very much in it.

"Please, have a seat."

They perched themselves on the extreme edge of an ivory cream sofa.

"Thank you, Mrs Fraser," Ryan said. "Perhaps you could tell us a bit more about the trouble with your car?"

She made herself comfortable on one of the matching chairs arranged around a glass coffee table and crossed her ankles. "Well, I was away for a few days at the spa," she said. "Actually, it was a present from Duncan; he surprised me with it on Friday. He can be so thoughtful when he wants to be, you know. It's a pity he couldn't come, but he drove me down to the spa hotel so I wouldn't have to drive myself."

"He sounds like the ideal husband," Phillips said.

"Oh, he *is*. I had the most marvellous few days, and I felt *so* relaxed. That is, until Duncan came along to collect me yesterday in that beat up old Defender he refuses to part with, rather than our new Range Rover Evoque—which is far more comfortable for my back, you know—and told me the Range Rover had been stolen from right under our noses."

They made a note of the registration plate, make, model and colour.

"So, you believe the car was stolen while you were away?"

"Yes, Duncan thinks it must have happened during the early hours of yesterday morning, but we keep it parked around the corner, so he only realised it had gone when he went to get the car later in the day."

Ryan's mind raced back to the information they'd already gathered. Unfortunately, no black Range Rover Evoque had been seen anywhere near the Golf Club in Dunstanburgh, and nobody in attendance happened to drive that particular model. He decided to check whether any old Defenders had been sighted, just in case.

"This kind of thing really shouldn't happen to a Member of Parliament, you know," she continued, as if they alone were responsible. "Why hasn't the car been found yet? You can't expect an MP to get around his constituency on his bike."

"Your husband rides, does he?" Phillips asked.

"Oh, yes," she said, dismissively. "He's always off up the coast, or out in the Tynedale Valley on his bike. He says it's good exercise, which I suppose it is."

"Actually, I'm a bit of a cyclist myself—" Phillips began.

"Coming back to the car," Ryan interjected. "Do you know if any spare keys have gone missing?"

Just then, they heard the outer door opening.

"Ellie! I'm back!"

"Through here, Duncan!" she called out, obviously pleased to know he'd returned.

A moment later, a tall, attractive man of around her own age entered the living room wearing a smartly tailored suit in navy blue.

"Here you are—"

He caught sight of their visitors, and stopped dead.

"Oh, Duncan, this is perfect timing," his wife said. "These two gentlemen are from Northumbria CID; they're here to talk about the car."

"Amongst other things," Ryan said, and rose to his feet. "Pleased to meet you, Mr Fraser."

He held out a hand, which the MP shook after an infinitesimal pause.

"Well," he said. "Good. *Good*. I'm glad you've come, although I'm sorry to have put you to any trouble. I know how hard you work in the Constabulary. In fact, last time I was in the House, I lobbied the Prime Minister and the Justice Minister to make more funds available—"

"We're always grateful for the chance to do our jobs better," Ryan cut in, smoothly. "Now you're here, perhaps you can help us by providing some information?"

Fraser looked at his wife, then back again.

"Well, I don't know what more I can add to the statement I gave your colleagues yesterday," he said. "I simply dropped Eleanor off at the spa on Friday, then went to a planned dinner with my staff from the constituency office here in town. On Saturday, I had a number of appointments throughout the day, and another dinner in the evening, this time with members of our local Chamber of Commerce. On Sunday, I gave a speech at a charity fundraising event, followed by a long lunch. I have a driver who chauffeurs me between engagements, so I had no need to drive a car myself until yesterday when I was due to collect Eleanor."

"What time did you go out, intending to retrieve your car, Mr Fraser?"

"Oh, it must have been around ten o'clock yesterday morning. The plan was for me to meet Eleanor at the spa hotel for around twelve, since it's roughly two hours away, have a spot of lunch together and then drive home afterwards."

"So thoughtful, as always," she chimed in, and he patted her cheek in a manner Ryan found vaguely nauseating.

"I assume the car went missing late on Sunday night or early on Monday morning," Fraser continued, slipping an arm around his wife's waist. "Any would-be thieves would be under cover of darkness."

"Do you have CCTV in the area?" Phillips asked him.

"Sadly, not," Fraser replied. "We have CCTV to protect the house, of course, but there's nothing on the street. It's a lesson to us for next time, isn't it, darling?"

"Well, I did ask if it was a good idea to move the cars, didn't I?" she said, teasingly. "I don't know why you thought they'd be safer around there, when we've always had them parked in front of the house."

Panic flickered in the man's eyes. "Kids," he said. "They cut through here all the time, on their way to the bars and pubs on the High Street. I can't tell you how many times the paintwork has been scratched, or the alarm's gone off. I thought it would reduce the chances of that happening so often if I simply moved the cars out of the main throughfare."

"Of course," Ryan said, all smoothness again. "That makes perfect sense."

"Well, if you don't have any update as to its whereabouts," Fraser said. "We best let you hardworking officers get back to more important matters—"

He began to usher them out, but Ryan remained standing where he was.

"Speaking of more important matters, Mr Fraser, we'd like to speak to you about something else. Mrs Fraser? I'm afraid this is confidential, so we must ask you to give us some privacy."

She looked at her husband, who nodded.

"It's all right, dear. This is probably about one of my constituents, and they're quite right to protect that person's privacy. I'll come and join you in a minute."

Ryan thanked her again and, once the door had firmly closed, faced the elephant in the room. He cited the standard caution for Duncan Fraser who was, they noted, beginning to sweat profusely.

"Should I be calling a solicitor?" he asked.

"That's entirely at your discretion," Ryan said. "However, we're simply asking some basic questions regarding one of our ongoing investigations. We can, of course, move this to the station and wait for your solicitor to arrive."

Fraser thought of the press, of his wife and his girlfriend, and shook his head. "No, no," he said, all smiles again. "I'm happy to assist however I can."

"In that case, does the name Will Harding mean anything to you?"

Fraser began to shrug out of his blazer jacket, the temperature in the room having jumped significantly. "Not especially," he said. "Why?"

"He's a photographer," Ryan pressed him. "You're sure that you don't know him?"

Fraser transformed into the charming 'man of the people' they recognised from the television. "As I'm sure you can appreciate, I meet an awful lot of photographers," he said. "I'm photographed almost daily, and I couldn't hope to remember the names of every one of them."

"This one happens to be dead," Ryan said.

Fraser did not react, except to offer his belated sympathies. "I'm very sorry to hear that, of course—and my condolences to his family."

Ryan turned to Phillips, who retrieved the photographic files and turned his smartphone around so that Fraser could see them on the screen for himself.

"Do you recognise this photograph, Mr Fraser?"

He turned white, first, and then a slow shade of red.

"Or this one?" Phillips asked, flipping to the next.

"*Get out*," Fraser snarled, flying into a sudden rage. "Take your filthy pictures with you! And mark my words, if a single one of them find their way to the press, I'll have your jobs. You can count on it! Now, get out of my house, before I have you thrown out!"

Unmoved by the outburst, Ryan leaned forward and looked the man dead in the eye. "Nobody is above the law," he said softly. "Not even you."

They left him to think about it.

CHAPTER 23

As the door slammed shut behind them, Ryan turned to his sergeant. "Let's go for a walk, Frank. I need to think."

Phillips nodded. "So long as the walk includes a takeaway cuppa, I'm all for it."

"That goes without saying."

They made their way through the upmarket residential streets of Gosforth in the direction of the high street, which was quiet now that the lunchtime crowd had gone back to their homes and desks. After a brief stop into a coffee shop, they continued past the shops and cut through a small shopping centre until they reached the entrance to the park.

"Pinter sent through his initial thoughts on the farmer's wife," Ryan said, as they made their way around its pathways, dodging an interminable stream of buggies and scooters with the kind of aplomb shown only by those with experience of small children.

"Oh aye? What does he have to say?"

They came to an empty bench and seated themselves, looking out across the bowling green.

"As we predicted, Kath Hopkins suffered major trauma to her vital organs following head-on impact, which would have been life-threatening, in any case. But it was the blow to the back of her head that killed her, in Pinter's view."

Phillips nodded and took a sip of green tea. "Faulkner seemed to think there were three separate head injuries," he said.

"Pinter agrees with him but can't say with any certainty whether they'd have been inflicted by an assailant or caused by being thrown into the air after impact with the car. It's too close to call."

"The tracks, though?"

Ryan stretched out his legs and crossed them at the ankles, eyes narrowed as he thought not of children playing on the swings, nor of dogs chasing sticks, but of a woman left to die out on a bleak road in Northumberland.

"The tracks on the verge are indisputable, according to Faulkner. The car impacted, then reversed away again. There were drag marks across the tarmac to indicate the body was moved, and we know from the degree of her injuries and the way she was found, Kath couldn't possibly have dragged herself to the middle of the road. Therefore, someone had their hands on her."

"Those same hands could have inflicted the fatal blows," Phillips said, and looked across at his friend.

"My thoughts exactly. Low Copy Number DNA is being analysed from that site, as well as the site up at the Golf Club—"

"You're linking Harding and Hopkins?" Phillips said, with surprise. "There's no suggestion those two deaths are connected, is there?"

Ryan smiled, grimly. "I didn't think there was, until half an hour ago," he said. "But get this: Faulkner found traces of some unidentified white powder, as well as black paint they recovered from Kath's belt, which must have transferred on impact."

He looked over at his sergeant. "It's entirely coincidental, and, at the moment, there is absolutely no connection I could put in front of the Crown Prosecution Service, but...Frank, what colour was the Fraser's stolen car?"

"Black," Phillips said. "And it was supposedly stolen during the relevant timescale when Kath died."

"Duncan Fraser's counsel would say that his car was stolen and used to commit murder by person or persons unknown—which might still be true."

"But?" Phillips prompted.

"He's a lying bastard," Ryan said, conversationally. "He lies to his wife; he lies to us, or omits to tell us about knowing Will Harding; and everything in my gut is telling me he's lying about that bloody car. I have to wonder what else he's trying to hide."

Phillips nodded. "As far as I know, Jack and Charlie haven't made any further progress with the Harding case in Embleton," he said. "I had a message from Jack earlier to say they're nearing the end of their interview list, but nobody so far has raised a red flag. The only clear link we have is between two dead men: Harding and Atherton. Even then, it doesn't translate to murder."

"And now we have a potential link between Harding and Fraser, although I can't see any possible reason why Fraser would concern himself with Kath Hopkins, except that her husband, Alan, was very vocal against local government," Ryan said, and let out a short sigh that was pure frustration. "We need more information or all of this is just theories and pie in the sky. Has Mac made any progress on the Atherton case?"

"She spoke to his old boss at *The Daily Chronicle* this morning, along with a few of Atherton's old workmates, but none of them know of him having had any relationship with Will Harding. They know the name, they've seen his photography work, but they have a couple of regular press photographers they tend to use and have done for years. It's very unlikely Atherton would have gone outside and hired Harding for professional reasons."

It was as they'd expected, but it didn't help their case.

"Anything else?"

"Actually, Denise said she was waiting to hear back from Atherton's internet provider with his browsing history," Phillips said. "That could be interesting—"

"Damn," Ryan said, as his phone began to vibrate.

The number on the screen belonged to the Chief Constable.

He thought seriously about ignoring the call, but good judgment and a keen sense of self-preservation forced him to answer instead.

Immediately, he regretted his decision.

After a chilling exchange with Chief Constable Morrison, Ryan and Phillips hot-footed it back to Police Headquarters as fast as modern transport and early afternoon traffic would carry them. When they presented themselves outside her corner office on the Executive Floor, a new personal assistant by the name of Pooja awaited them with a Sphynx-like smile.

"Go straight in," she said, without needing to ask who they were. "They're expecting you."

"They?" Phillips whispered.

"*They*," she repeated, and jabbed a fingernail towards the door.

Ryan squared his shoulders, Phillips made the sign of the cross on his own chest, and then raised a knuckle for a peremptory knock.

"Come in."

Ryan stepped over the threshold and into the domain of the Chief Constable. Having worked together for a number of years, he knew Sandra Morrison to be a fair woman and, most crucially, not one to bow under pressure as a general rule. On the other hand, her role was as much a political and diplomatic one as it was that of a senior police officer; it was she who liaised with, cajoled, managed and misdirected those in positions of power, so that her people on the ground dealing with front-line policing could get their jobs done which, ultimately, brought results. It was a thankless job, and he never underestimated it, but there were times when she was torn between her professional friendships and the job she'd signed up to do.

On that particular day, the balance was precarious.

Upon entering the room, the first thing Ryan and Phillips noticed was not the relatively diminutive figure of their Chief Constable, but the same navy-blue suit they'd seen an hour before, worn by none other than Duncan Fraser, MP. He was joined by another man in a dark suit, who wore glasses and a pocket square, and they weren't smiling.

Neither was Morrison.

"Ryan, Phillips, thank you for joining us at short notice," she said crisply, and without any of the usual pleasantries they'd come to expect.

"We came as quickly as we could, ma'am," Ryan said, and then took the bull by the horns. "Mr Fraser, it's good to see you again so soon. I presume you've come with your lawyer to make a formal statement about your relationship with Will Harding?"

Fraser's lawyer opened his mouth but was intercepted.

"Sit *down*, the pair of you," Morrison said, between gritted teeth.

They obeyed her command.

"You already know Mr Fraser," she said. "And, yes, you're quite right, this is his lawyer, Frederick Henderson, of Henderson & Henderson, LLP."

It was the premier legal firm in the North, and Henderson was one of its founding partners, which told them two things: first, that they'd really managed to set the cat amongst the pigeons; and, second, that Duncan Fraser had Fred Henderson on speed dial, to be able to elicit his help within the space of an hour.

Excellent, Ryan thought.

"I understand you attended Mr Fraser's home and spoke to his wife under false pretences, following which you harassed Mr Fraser about the death of a photographer before making defamatory insinuations about his private life. Is that correct?"

Ryan eyed the man across the room, who was looking decidedly cockier than he had when they'd left him sweating and fuming in his front room.

"Of course it isn't true."

"Now he's accusing me of lying?" Fraser burst out, and turned to his solicitor. "My integrity is unimpeachable. This is an *outrage*—"

"We attended Mr Fraser's home in connection with some highly compromising photographs, which were found on the hard drive of a photographer by the name of William Harding, who was murdered last Friday," Ryan overrode him with ease. "The images show Mr Fraser with an unidentified blonde woman, and we were within the bounds of our investigation to question him about it."

"At this juncture, my client would like to remind you of the relevant Data Protection legislation," Henderson interjected. "As I'm sure you're aware, the provisions prevent public disclosure of sensitive personal data of this kind, and my client is also covered by the relevant exemptions which apply to Members of Parliament."

He took out a photocopy of the legislation, which Ryan knew by rote.

"My client has been a longstanding advocate for our Police Service, and hopes this discussion will put an end to this unpleasant matter," Henderson continued, in a tone laced with just enough condescension to put their hackles up. "I'm sure we'd all like to put this behind us."

He paused, for dramatic effect.

"However, I must warn you that, should any of my client's imagery find its way into the public domain, we will not hesitate to seek reparations and will prosecute to the fullest extent of the law."

On which note, he turned to Morrison.

"I'm assured by my client that he is a forgiving man, with a stellar reputation," he said. "If we are in receipt of a full, written apology by close of business today, and no further harassment is forthcoming, he will consider the matter closed."

Sandra Morrison was a seasoned police officer of many years' good standing, and needed no tutelage in the application of legislation they used and worked around every day. However, she relied on her staff to know whether they had exceeded its bounds on any case-by-case basis, and therefore she looked to Ryan, who was only too happy to answer her unspoken question.

"I'm afraid we won't be issuing an apology today," he said, and came to his feet. "Thank you for drawing my attention to the Data Protection legislation, Mr Henderson; you've called to mind an important point which, I fear, you may have overlooked."

The man bristled, while Fraser's eyes darted between the two of them.

"What point?" he asked.

Henderson put a staying hand on his arm, and raised an imperious eyebrow. "I hardly think so, but please, do enlighten me."

Ryan picked up the sheet of paper with the excerpt of the Regulations printed on it, and, very calmly, crumpled it in his fist before lobbing it into the wastepaper basket.

"The provisions of the Regulations apply only to living, identifiable persons. Therefore, it only applies if the MP is accepting that he is the man in the photographs—since you've spent the past five minutes detailing the ways in which these provisions do apply, I must assume your client accepts he is the subject of them. As for any exclusions relating to Members of Parliament, my understanding is that they apply only to activities carried out in the course of his work as an MP. Is it your position that the activities in those images constituted official Parliamentary business?"

There was a short, pregnant silence.

"My client has nothing further to add," Henderson said, once he'd pulled himself together. "This isn't an interview—"

"I'd be more than happy to show your client the interview suite, downstairs."

"I—"

"Phillips? Show Mr Fraser and Mr Henderson the way." Ryan turned to his Chief Constable. "Good afternoon, ma'am."

"Tread carefully," she warned him, and Ryan nodded.

As the door shut behind them, Morrison sat back down at her desk, smiled privately to herself, and then moved onto the next fire that required fighting.

CHAPTER 24

"DCI Ryan and DS Phillips entering Interview Room 2. Also present are Duncan Fraser, Member of Parliament, and Frederick Henderson, his legal counsel, of Henderson & Henderson, Newcastle upon Tyne."

Ryan gave the date and time, as well as the standard caution, for the benefit of the tape recording that would capture their interview.

"Do you understand your rights and obligations, Mr Fraser?"

The latter had a face like thunder, and gave a brief nod.

"If you would kindly answer clearly, 'yes' or 'no', for the benefit of the tape," Ryan said.

"*Yes*," the man snapped.

"Good. Now, we'd like to ask you some questions in connection with a series of photographic images, date-stamped"—he paused to refer to his file, and gave the precise time and date they were taken—"and found on the external hard drive at an address belonging to the late William Harding, who, at the time of this interview, died only a few days ago. Firstly, can you tell me whether you know Mr Harding?"

Fraser, who had spent the past twenty minutes in a conference room with his solicitor, folded his arms across his chest and eyed them both with contempt.

"No comment."

Ryan merely smiled.

"My client would like me to read out a statement," Henderson said.

"We're all ears," Phillips said.

"Very well then. Mr Fraser wishes me to say that, approximately four months ago, and to his great regret, he participated in a one-off romantic liaison with his constituency office coordinator whilst they were both in attendance at a festive event over the Christmas period—"

"Do you have the address of the venue where your client had sex with his secretary whilst at their Christmas party?" Ryan said, mildly.

Fraser glared at him, but kept his counsel.

"The address is hardly relevant—" Henderson said.

"On the contrary, it is very relevant to our investigation," Ryan said.

Henderson leaned in to speak with Fraser, who lifted a shoulder and whispered something in his ear.

"My client is willing to provide the address," he said, and rattled off the name of a swanky hotel on the outskirts of the city. "To continue his statement, Mr Fraser denies having seen any of these photographs before today, and denies any knowledge of the person who took them without his consent. That is all he has to say on the matter."

Ryan began to say something, when Phillips placed a hand on his arm and leaned in to speak in an undertone.

"They've found the Range Rover," he whispered.

Ryan nodded, and then spoke again. "Interview terminated at fourteen-oh-seven," he said, and began to gather his things.

"Just a minute." Henderson scrambled to get up. "Don't you have anything to say?"

Ryan lanced him with a single look. "Not for now," he said, and turned to go, before thinking better of it. "Mr Fraser, you're a bit strapped for transport at the moment. Do you need a lift?"

Fraser scraped back his chair, ready to issue a furious rebuttal.

"No?" Ryan said. "All right, then. Enjoy your day in the sunshine; you never know how long it'll last."

"Was it wise to goad him like that?"

Phillips polished off a ham and cheese croissant, and brushed the crumbs from his knees as they made their way west of the city, to a lay-by four miles away from where Kath Hopkins' body was discovered. The route took them along a long road known as the 'Military Road', which ran almost parallel to Hadrian's Wall.

"I want him rattled," Ryan said, as they flew around another bend. "I need Duncan Fraser to keep sweating and worrying, because sweaty, worried people make mistakes."

Phillips grinned. "You've got an evil streak a mile wide," he said. "It narf makes me proud."

They turned off the main road and along a single track that would take them a cross-country route towards Housesteads Roman fort. They bounced over rough track until they spotted a squad car parked up ahead, alongside a black Range Rover that appeared to have been abandoned in a passing point in the road, and, beyond that, Faulkner's black van.

"I don't know how he always beats us to it," Phillips said.

"Because I called him the moment we left the Interview Suite," Ryan said. "He didn't need to stop for French pastry, unlike some I could mention."

"I'm packin' on the protein," Phillips said, indignantly. "That's what all the bodybuilders do, before they shred off the fat and reveal a six-pack that's been lurkin' underneath. I'm carb-loadin', too, because I've got this Dance-Off to think about, and the last thing I need is to run out of energy."

"So many questions," Ryan muttered. "So little time. Sadly, they'll have to wait."

They parked alongside the squad car, exchanged a word with the constable who was seated inside, and then headed over to where Faulkner was inspecting the interior of the Range Rover.

"Tom, what can you tell us?"

Faulkner glanced back over his shoulder and then extracted himself from the driver's side. "First things first, you can see from the state of the windows and the interior that the airbags were deployed on impact," he said, and they looked behind him to see the remains of what looked like an explosion of flour. "That tells us a couple of things. For starters, the car hit Kath Hopkins with sufficient speed to deploy—"

"God rest her," Phillips murmured.

The other two nodded.

"The powder comes from the coating on the airbags, so they remain functional despite being stored for years without being used," Faulkner continued. "But the more interesting point is how the powder managed to transfer itself from the interior of the car onto Kath's body."

They were quick studies.

"The windshield and other car windows are intact," Ryan said, running his eyes over the vehicle a few metres away from where they huddled. "There isn't any feasible way the powder could have transferred itself onto Kath Hopkins on impact. Therefore, it could only have transferred when she was dragged into the middle of the road by whoever mowed her down."

Faulkner nodded.

"It's the most plausible explanation," he said. "Aside from the powder, we've got what looks like a match to the black paint recovered from her belt; you can see the slight indentation and a scrape along the bonnet."

"The registration plate's a match to the missing Range Rover reported as stolen by the Frasers," Phillips put in. "There's still a chance that thieves stole the car and ran her down, then abandoned it here."

"There's only a couple of partial prints on the driver's side of the vehicle," Faulkner said, and they walked back to the vehicle so he could point them out. "It was raining overnight, so that might have obscured any others there may have been. The only other track that's of interest is this one."

He moved to the rear of the car and pointed to the ground, where they saw a single, slim tyre track ran from the boot area across the muddy lay-by towards the road.

"Looks like a bicycle track to me," he said.

Ryan turned to Phillips. "Frank, who do we know that's an experienced cyclist, aside from your good self?"

The other man grinned. "The owner of that Range Rover, for a start," he replied. "Apparently, he loves a ride out in the countryside, too."

"Perhaps we should ask Mr Fraser where he's hidden his muddy bike—"

Just then, Ryan's phone began to ring. "It's Denise," he said, and answered it. "Mac?"

"Ryan, I need you both back at Police Headquarters," she said, in an urgent tone.

"We'll head back, as soon as we've finished going over this car—" he began.

"You don't understand," she said. "I've cracked it. I've found the key."

CHAPTER 25

An hour later, Ryan, Phillips, Lowerson and Reed converged upon Police Headquarters, where they found MacKenzie scribbling notes on a whiteboard in their usual conference room.

"Mac? What's going on?" Ryan demanded, as the door shut behind them.

She turned and pointed towards a short stack of photocopies that were still warm from the copier machine.

"Look at those," she said, and re-capped her pen.

Ryan snatched one up, skim-read the content, then looked up again in confusion. "Classified ads from *The Northern Fisherman*?" he said. "I don't follow."

MacKenzie took a seat, partly to settle her own nerves, and they followed her example.

"Wait a minute," Charlie said, suddenly. "There's an ad here listed by Will Harding, from last December—"

"And another by Kath Hopkins," Phillips said, and looked amongst his friends. "What's goin' on?"

"I received a full listing of Marcus Atherton's browsing history for the past six months from his ISP, earlier today," MacKenzie told them. "I spent most of the day trawling through it, and comparing their data against the browsing history stored on Atherton's phone and home computer. As we suspected, there were discrepancies. In particular, there was some key activity surrounding this one publication, *The Northern Fisherman* missing from his search history."

MacKenzie passed around a document she'd produced which showed an abridged listing of the missing searches.

"Before you look at it, just humour me for a minute," she said. "Take out your phones, and open up a search engine."

They followed her instruction without question.

"Now, type in, 'ANDREA PETERSON, NEWBIGGIN-BY-THE-SEA'," she said.

They did as she told them, and watched a series of results flash up on their screens. The top one was an obituary in *The Daily Chronicle*; next, a couple of mentions on social media sites, and, finally, the fourth listing was a classified ad in *The Northern Fisherman*.

Ryan looked back at MacKenzie.

"Andrea Peterson?"

"Died, October last year," she said. "Now, delete that search, and try another one. This time, type in, 'MOHAMMED KHAN, DENTON BURN', and see what comes up."

They followed her instruction again, and found another listing in *The Northern Fisherman*.

Sale of gear offered by Mohammed Khan, must collect in person from Denton Burn.

"Before you ask, Mohammed Khan died in September of last year," she said. "Now, look at the photocopies of the classifieds for the December edition of the magazine again, and also the classifieds which went out at the end of last month."

With a sick feeling in his stomach, Ryan reached for the piece of paper and re-read the words printed there.

Sale of gear offered by Will Harding, Central Newcastle, one of them read. *Must be collected by April, latest.*

And then, from the most recent edition of the magazine:

Seeking new gear, please contact Kath Hopkins, Chollerford, by the end of the month.

He set the paper down on the desk again, and steepled his fingers while his mind raced with possibilities, none of which were good.

"How far back?" he asked her.

"I need Jack and Charlie to help me go back as far as possible," she said. "I've made a start, but there are too many cold cases, suicides, and accidental deaths to be able to compare with the back issues of this magazine in the space of a few hours. I was able to find those two names, in addition to our open cases, but there could be many more."

"We'll get onto it straight away," Jack said, and Charlie could only nod her agreement.

Ryan pushed away from the table and walked to the window, where he looked out across the rooftops of the city.

"You think Atherton found this pattern?" he asked, turning back to look at MacKenzie.

"You can see from the browsing history that was subsequently deleted, Atherton probably picked up on an increase in accidental deaths and suicides over the past year or so, just as we have," she replied. "*The Northern Fisherman* has recently become digitized, so he might have been searching the names of the dead, alongside their addresses, perhaps to see if there was anything to uncover for an article... who knows. He must have found exactly what we've just discovered, which is that, when you search certain names, they come up in these classified listings, and, a week or so after, they wind up dead—either as accidents, suicides, or unsolved."

"He thought it was to do with the Circle," Ryan said quietly. "He came to us—to Frank and me—while we were on that case up at Lady's Well, and I thought at the time he was behaving oddly. I planned to follow up but then, the next thing I heard, he was dead."

"Your instincts were right, as always," Lowerson said. "You knew something wasn't right, and you wouldn't let us drop the case. You knew."

Ryan sighed and looked back out of the window to see the sun spreading its late afternoon haze across the people of Newcastle.

"I can't quite bring myself to celebrate," he muttered, and moved across to grip the back of one of the chairs while he processed the reality now facing them.

They waited, and, just for a moment, Charlie thought she felt the forcefield shift.

Then, Ryan looked up, and his eyes burned silver.

"No wonder we couldn't find any obvious motive for any of the people at Dunstanburgh Golf Club to kill Will Harding," he said. "It's because none of them have one. Who does? Duncan Fraser, who's in the running for ministerial office and can't afford any scandal, but also can't afford to keep paying escalating blackmail demands to a photographer who has the power to bring down his entire house of sand."

He pushed away from the chair and picked up MacKenzie's pen, which he used to draw lines to connect the names of the victims she'd listed on the whiteboard.

"Duncan Fraser has an airtight alibi for the time Harding was murdered," he continued. "The only person with any obvious motive, so far, couldn't possibly have done it, therefore we assume somebody else executed the murder on his order."

Ryan stood back from the board, and then tapped a finger on Kath Hopkin's name.

"In the case of our most recent victim, we couldn't find anyone with motive, means and opportunity to kill a woman who, by all accounts, had never harmed a soul in her life. The only person in possession of a decent motive is her husband, Alan Hopkins—"

"Who also had an airtight alibi," Phillips said, putting the jigsaw together. "He was in hospital under constant supervision, all night, and his halfwit friend didn't have access to a vehicle and was himself accounted for by his flatmate for the time Kath Hopkins died."

"Exactly," Ryan said. "Alan is heavily in debt and on the verge of losing his farm. He's already lost his wife, who's been having an affair with his old friend and has checked out of the marriage. He's off the rails, alcoholic, and she's in possession of a life insurance policy worth a quarter of a million."

"That'll do it," Phillips said. "But he's not the one who kills her."

"No," Ryan said. "It's Duncan Fraser's vehicle that hit her, and, I believe, Duncan Fraser who got out of that same vehicle, dragged Kath Hopkins into the middle of the road and cracked her skull against the tarmac to finish the job. I think he then reversed, drove around her and for another four miles until he found a side road that was off the beaten track. He then abandoned his vehicle, took out his mountain bike, and cycled home as the world was awakening."

"So…Fraser has no connection with Kath Hopkins whatsoever?" Charlie said, wrapping her head around the facts.

Ryan shook his head. "None whatsoever," he said.

"I have a question," Charlie said, and they turned to her. "I can see how Duncan Fraser could afford to pay for a hit, but how could Alan afford it? He doesn't have any money to pay someone to kill his wife."

Ryan drew another line on the whiteboard, this time connecting Fraser to Hopkins.

"He could have promised a share of the life insurance," he said. "But I think what we have here is a game of *quid pro quo*. Person A wants Person B dead, for whatever reason. They make contact with whoever is orchestrating this entire operation, who sets out the terms of engagement then places an ad in *The Northern Fisherman* detailing the name of their chosen victim, geographic location, and a rough timescale in which the assassination will happen. Money might be exchanged; we have no way of knowing right now, but, given the facts at our disposal, it seems that the idea is to receive a murder in exchange for committing one ordered by someone else. The participants may never know about each other until after the fact."

"So, Person A gets their wish, because Person C, another participant in the scheme, kills Person B. However, Person A may then be called upon at any time to reciprocate for Person D, E, F or whatever, at some point in the future?" Lowerson reasoned.

Ryan nodded.

"They get their wish, and there is likely some communication to let them know when the murder is planned to happen, so they can cover themselves and make sure they have a full alibi," he said. "Then, at some later date, they are then asked to take their turn and do someone else's bidding. They have to make their own arrangements, but they have a degree of natural cover, because the whole point is that they will have no connection at all with the intended victim, who they'll be setting up to look like an accident or a suicide, in any case."

"My God," MacKenzie murmured. "This could be enormous. There are thousands of accidental deaths on the system, for a start."

"That's just up here, in our constabulary," Phillips said. "What if this is a national cooperative, or whatever you want to call it? There could be hundreds of small, obscure magazines being used for the same purpose."

"Why do you think they publicise it at all?" Lowerson asked. "I don't understand why they would want to put anything in writing that could draw attention to the scheme?"

"Viability," MacKenzie answered, taking the words out of Ryan's mouth. "It proves to potential participants that the scheme is real, and therefore worthy of their investment."

"It also explains why Atherton made that call to Will Harding," Ryan added. "He must have seen the December edition of the magazine, where Harding's name was listed in the classifieds, and tried to warn him."

"Who killed Harding?" Charlie asked.

Ryan cocked his head, and managed a half-smile. "Who do you think?"

"The Club Secretary," she answered, without pause. "Jack and I were discussing this earlier and, now that we know the methodology, it makes even more sense. John Dawson is the one who hired Harding to attend a party he'd organised—therefore he had oversight of every detail, from the timings to the dates and everything else. He probably clubbed him around the back of the head inside one of the cupboards in that utility corridor, and locked him inside until the party was over."

"Dawson's the one with the keys," Lowerson said.

"He probably waited until the clubhouse had emptied, then dragged the body to the end of the corridor and out the back door into a waiting golf buggy. After that, it's just a case of driving down to the thirteenth tee and choosing a spot to dump him."

"He would have used Harding's finger to access his smartphone and delete anything incriminating," Jack reminded her, and she nodded.

"We might think we know what's happenin' but we still don't have enough proof to charge any of them," MacKenzie said.

"In the meantime, there's every chance another name will be advertised in that bloody fishing rag," Phillips said. "What do we do about it?"

A short, tense silence followed in which Ryan felt their eyes upon him, waiting for him to deliver the leadership they had come to expect.

"It's getting on for five o'clock," he said, and made sure his voice gave away nothing of his own fear. "Charlie? I know you need to get home to your son, so that's what you should do. Frank? Denise? I want you to do the same. Go home, be with your daughter—"

"I'm going nowhere till we get to the bottom of this," Phillips replied, resolutely.

"All right—we're going to pay a visit to the editor of this publication, as soon as I've spoken with the Chief Constable. Jack—"

"I'll start going through the cold cases," he said quietly, and Ryan nodded his thanks.

They disbanded and, left briefly alone in the empty conference room, Ryan took a moment to rest his forehead against the back of the door, the weight of responsibility heavy upon his shoulders.

For how could you fight, when you didn't know who your foe was?

It was a terrifying prospect—and they were only just beginning.

CHAPTER 25

The sun had fallen low in the sky by the time Ryan and Phillips made their way out of the city towards Morpeth. It was a pretty market town, located off the A1 motorway fifteen or so miles north of Newcastle, and was home to the editor of *The Northern Fisherman,* a man by the name of Greg Pulteney.

"D' you think he's the one behind it all?" Phillips asked, as they came off the slip road.

Ryan followed the directions listed on his GPS and indicated left. "Too early to say," he replied. "Common sense would tell me, 'no', because it would be foolish to use your own magazine as the platform to advertise your alternative scheme, wouldn't it?"

Phillips nodded. "Not all killers are smart, but this isn't an ordinary killer," he said. "We're looking for someone with strategic planning… more like the CEO of a company."

"Or a non-profit, if they don't charge for the service," Ryan said, and felt his stomach quiver again. "That's infinitely more dangerous, because it provides an endless pool of possible killers who aren't reliant on having financial means."

Phillips looked across at his friend's profile, which might have been cast in granite. "There can't be many people who know about this…can there?"

Ryan said nothing, because there was nothing he *could* say. In cases of murder, or multiple murders, they would always be the last to know.

There was one thing he did know, and it gave little comfort. "There's a world full of good people, Frank. But there's a small minority who aren't like the rest; they aren't part of the same society, and don't conform to its norms. They'd kill, if they had the chance, but, normally, it's too risky for them to attempt it without being found out. Whoever has put this scheme together has taken inspiration from the very worst of human nature, providing the conditions to be able to do that which they might only dream of, in the darkest part of their hearts."

"Not everyone has it in them."

Ryan looked at his own hands, which gripped the steering wheel tightly, and thought of a time they were around a man's neck. "Depending on the circumstances, the opportunity, the loss of reason or desperation, everyone has it in them."

Before his friend could answer, they pulled into an estate of newly-built houses, arranged in a collection of cul-de-sacs.

"We're looking for Number 9," Ryan said.

Spotting it, he performed a swift parallel park, and the two men exited the car and made their way across the street, their footsteps clicking against the new pavement as they hurried towards Pulteney's front door.

Ryan leaned on the doorbell, and they heard a series of loud barks in response.

"Ssh! *Quiet!*"

A moment later, the door opened to reveal a man of around Ryan's age, who gripped the collar of what they'd expected to find was an enormous hound, but which was, in fact, a Pomeranian.

"Sorry about Lady Muck," he said, as she continued to yap. "She's a bit tetchy, today. Can I help you?"

"Mr Pulteney?"

"Yes?"

"We're DCI Ryan and DS Phillips, from Northumbria CID. We're investigating a series of suspected murders in the region, and believe you may be able to help us with some of our queries."

They held out their warrant cards, and watched him pale, visibly.

"I—I'm not under suspicion, am I? I haven't murdered anyone—"

"You're not under any suspicion at the present time, Mr Pulteney, but your magazine, *The Northern Fisherman* is of interest to us. May we come in?"

Pulteney still looked as though a strong wind could carry him off, but agreed without any complaint. "I—yes, yes, come in. I'm sorry, the place is a bit topsy-turvy at the moment."

He picked up Lady Muck, so that she wouldn't try to take a chunk out of their ankles, and they followed him down a small, narrow hallway that was covered in fishing paraphernalia from floor to ceiling.

"I'll just pop Lady back in her dog bed," he said. "Just wait in the lounge, and I'll be through in a minute. Do you want anything? Water? Tea?"

"No, thank you, we're fine."

He showed them into the lounge, which was similarly cluttered with books, fishing magazines, more fishing magazines and yet *more* fishing magazines, before disappearing off in the direction of the kitchen, where they heard him speaking to her in a soothing voice as he dished up some sort of dog treat.

"At least he seems to be a legitimate enthusiast," Ryan said, eyeing a collection of framed photographs featuring Pulteney holding enormous fish of varied description in his hands.

Before Phillips could respond, the man himself bustled back into the room. "Sorry to keep you," he said. "Please have a seat."

They saw no harm in it, and settled themselves on the sofa, while Pulteney took the chair facing them.

"Thank you for agreeing to help us, Mr Pulteney," Ryan began, having already identified him as a man who responded well to social etiquette.

"I'll be glad to, although I have to confess I'm completely in the dark as to what possible help I can give," he replied, looking genuinely confused. "I don't know of anyone in my circle who's died recently, let alone been murdered."

"Do you know a man named Will Harding?" Ryan asked, watching him closely.

Pulteney shook his head. "I don't think so, no—*no*! Hang on! I know a Will Harding who's a photographer, if that's who you mean? He does landscapes, I think, but he also does events and all kinds."

"How do you know him?"

"Oh, I don't, I'm just a member of a camera club and I see his name and a few of his pictures pop up on the Facebook group, sometimes—and I'm sure I've seen his name crop up elsewhere. Unless it's a different Will Harding that you're thinking of?"

Ryan ignored the question, and pressed on. "What about Kath Hopkins?"

Pulteney thought about it, then shook his head. "No, I don't think I know that name at all," he said. "Should I?"

Again, Ryan ignored the question. "Can you tell me who manages the 'classifieds' section of the magazine, please?"

"Oh, that would be Frederika," he said. "She's our intern."

"How long has she managed the classifieds?" Phillips asked.

"Only the last couple of editions," he replied. "It's a job we tend to give to the interns, so before Frederika it was Jamil, and before him it was Pippa. They all do three to six months taking care of the obituaries and the classifieds, until they get to grips with what it takes to run a magazine—then, of course, they move on to better things than a small fishing magazine!" He laughed, self-deprecatingly.

"Have you, yourself, ever dealt with the classifieds?"

Pulteney shook his head. "Not anymore," he said. "When I first started the magazine, I did everything myself, but that was…goodness, more than fifteen years ago, now. Time flies, doesn't it?"

"Yes, it does. If someone wished to place a classified ad, how would they go about it?"

"Well, it used to be that you had to call us up to pay over the phone and tell us the details of your ad, but nowadays it's all managed online; it's far simpler, that way. All anybody has to do is fill out an online form, and pay that way."

Ryan thought of the technological nightmare of having to trawl through what would undoubtedly turn out to be false names and false addresses, submitted from an untraceable server. It would be their next task to trace the source of the ads, unless he could find another way to approach the problem.

"How do you distribute the magazine, nowadays?"

"Well, we only have a small physical print circulation, as I'm sure you'll have guessed. We get a few copies out to the newsagents in the region, specialist shops, the occasional small supermarket and print subscriber...but mostly, we circulate digital copies to our subscribers. The numbers have been really encouraging, lately."

Ryan's ears pricked up. "Really?" he said. "Would you say the numbers of digital subscribers have increased lately?"

"Oh, definitely."

"Over what timescale, would you say?"

Pulteney scratched his chin. "Must be the past eighteen months, when I think about it," he said. "Why? Is that important?"

"It might be," Ryan said, studying the man before him. He came to a decision, and hoped it was the right one.

"I need your help, Mr Pulteney," he said, and leaned forward, forearms resting on his knees. "I could go away and seek a warrant, which would be the proper approach. However, time is very much of the essence, and further delay could cost lives."

Pulteney's eyes widened. "I understand—"

"I very much hope you *don't*," Ryan said, half to himself. "Otherwise, I'm not as good a judge of character as I thought. But, that aside, there is something we would very much appreciate, and that's your list of subscribers."

Pulteney's face fell. "Oh, dear…this is…it puts me in a bit of a position,' he muttered, thinking of the online GDPR and Data Protection training he'd recently completed. For anybody in the business of collecting personal data, the wrath of the Information Commissioner was nothing to be sniffed at.

On the other hand, the man sitting before him looked deadly serious.

"You said…it may cost lives?"

"I wouldn't lie to you, Mr Pulteney. We need that list urgently, as part of a serious criminal investigation—I promise you, if we were to have made a formal request in writing, it would meet the exemptions provided in the legislation."

Pulteney looked between Ryan and Phillips, and relied on his own good judgment.

"All right, then," he said. "Give me a few minutes, and I'll send you the spreadsheet. Your timing's pretty good, actually; our next issue goes out tomorrow morning."

Ryan stood, and took the unusual step of holding out a hand. "Thank you, Mr Pulteney."

He took the hand, and flushed with pleasure at the prospect of having been useful. "Not at all," he said, and turned to go in search of his laptop.

"Just one more thing," Phillips stopped him. "You haven't given the list of subscribers to anyone else, lately, have you?"

Pulteney looked insulted by the very thought.

"Absolutely not," he said. "I'm the only one with access to full administration rights, so none of our other staff would have the capability to share the information, even if they'd wanted to." He paused, suddenly understanding what they were really asking. "If you're wondering how someone might have come by the list, then it's possible they might have bribed the printers or distributers," he suggested. "There's many a slip between a cup and a lip, after all."

They thanked him and, once they were alone, Ryan turned to Phillips. "Atherton must have come by the subscriber list, somehow," he said.

"How do you know?"

"Because it's what I would have done, if I was him."

CHAPTER 26

Ryan and Phillips decided to split the list of subscribers to *The Northern Fisherman* between them, with a view to seeing whether the names included any that were already known to the police. Afterwards, they would need to cross-check the subscriber list against suspicious classified ad placements, to try to marry together the name of an advertiser against those adverts which included a suspected victim, such as Kath Hopkins or Will Harding. Given the surprisingly large number of subscribers to the magazine, the process was likely to be painstaking.

With these troubling thoughts circling, they left Greg Pulteney to his fish and headed back to their car, where Ryan settled himself in the driver's side but didn't start the engine. Outside, the sun had almost disappeared off the edge of the earth, and the skies over Northumberland were awash with colour, so he sat quietly for a moment and watched the shifting clouds.

"It's a beautiful world, isn't it, Frank?"

Phillips linked his fingers over his paunch. "Aye, it is," he agreed. "Even when we're dealin' with all these crackpots and fruitcakes, the world's still a lovely place to be. They're the minority, in any case."

Ryan said nothing to that, but tapped his phone, which contained the e-mail Pulteney had sent attaching his list of subscribers. "What kind of person does this, Frank? Who'd think of creating a killing scheme? It's beyond comprehension."

Phillips considered his friend, and worried about the weight of expectation he carried—for himself, and for others. For all his experience dealing with the worst of humanity, Ryan still asked himself, 'why', because he remained an idealist to the core. He questioned the destruction, the malice, and all the other ways in which one person could harm another, because he wasn't built the same as some people were. He thought the *best* of others, even when they didn't think it of themselves, and it was something that both inspired and saddened, in equal measure; because, to place humanity on a pedestal was to be perennially disappointed.

"They're *not* a real person, lad. Nobody who wants to be a part of society, and live in peace rather than fear and anarchy, would think to do somethin' like this. It's evil, if you want to call it that."

Ryan nodded, and flipped the sunscreen down to block the last rays of the sun, which were causing his eyes to blur. "I keep hoping, every time we find one and remove their ability to hurt people…I hope it's the last," he murmured. "I know—I *know*—it's a foolish, unrealistic hope, because as soon as you pluck a weed, another one springs straight up to take its place. There'll always be somebody else to do the killing, the raping, the assault, the stealing…you name it."

Phillips could only remind him of why he continued to pluck the weeds. "Without you and me, and all the others who stand for what's good and right in the world, they'd have free rein," Phillips said. "You can't change how other people think, or what they do, but you can try to prevent them from doing it again, that's for sure. You can protect the public from further harm."

Ryan looked across at Phillips, and managed a smile. "Thanks," he said, and turned on the engine. "I needed to hear that."

"Howay, lad. We'll not find anythin' more tonight," Phillips said. "Let's go and see our families, and fight the baddies again tomorrow."

Ryan thought of tomorrow, and of all the tomorrows that would never come for Will Harding and Kath Hopkins. "I won't rest easy until this one is behind us," he said. "It feels as though we've only touched the tip of the iceberg."

With a sharp flick of the wrist, Ryan turned the engine off again. "I have to see," he muttered, and Phillips heaved a sigh as Ryan brought up the spreadsheet on his phone.

"What d' you think you're goin' to see, lad? There're thousands of names on that list—"

"I'm looking for one in particular."

Phillips came to attention again. "Who?"

Ryan's fingers hovered over the keys as he poised to enter a name into the 'search' box. "Marcus Atherton asked me a question, before he died. He wanted to know if our case bore any resemblance to the style of murders committed by members of The Circle. I told him, 'no', because that group was disbanded, and the case didn't bear the same hallmarks. But, knowing what we do now, I have to wonder whether Atherton had a point."

"About The Circle?"

"Yes," Ryan said. "Not about The Circle having reformed, but about the similarity in organisational style. Here, you've got a cooperative where perfect strangers provide the means for one another, so those with the motive are beyond suspicion. It's circular."

"You reckon Atherton looked at the two and thought it was history repeatin' itself?"

Ryan nodded. "I'm also wondering whether he saw a name on this list that gave him reason to be so specific in his theory about The Circle. Perhaps he saw a name he recognised from the past."

Phillips sucked in a deep breath and let it out slowly. "Can't be," he said.

Ryan typed in a single name, and clicked, 'ENTER'.

There, in bold black lettering, was a subscriber named Arthur Gregson, resident of His Majesty's Prison Frankland.

It was almost ten o'clock by the time Ryan arrived home, having first put in a request to the governor of Frankland Prison for an interview with one of their Category A inmates the following morning. He'd spent a further two hours poring over the old file on their former Detective Chief Superintendent, Arthur Gregson, who'd been convicted of numerous criminal charges several years before.

Eventually, sickened by the memories, Ryan had called it a day.

A light burned in the hallway, as it always did when Anna knew he would be returning after nightfall. He toed off his boots and padded quietly towards the kitchen, where he found his wife sitting at the table yawning over a stack of essay papers she was working her way through marking, presumably for the students she taught a couple of days a week in the History Faculty of Durham University. The radio was turned down low, for background noise and company, so she didn't hear him, at first.

Ryan leaned against the doorframe to watch her for a moment, admiring the glossy sheen to her dark hair and the curve of her neck; her slim fingers as she scribbled a note on one of the papers and long eyelashes swept down over the curve of her cheek.

Suddenly, she looked up, and brown eyes met steel blue.

"Hello," he said simply.

Anna wondered if all people who were in love felt as she did, which was a feeling of renewal every time they were reunited. At the start of each new day, she fell for Ryan all over again, or even after just a few hours spent apart. Some people would laugh at her romantic notions, she supposed, and call her foolish.

Some people weren't lucky enough to be in love.

She crossed the kitchen and found herself wrapped in a pair of strong arms. "I missed you," she said.

In reply, he captured her mouth, one hand cradling her head while the other held her tightly against the hard wall of his body. His kiss was urgent, demanding, and was met in equal measure while their hands touched and explored the lines of their bodies, the feel of their skin.

"I love you," he muttered against her mouth.

"I love you, too."

He hoisted her up, wrapping her legs around his waist. "Time for bed?" he asked.

"Stop talking and take me upstairs."

He grinned against her neck, kissed the sensitive skin he found there, and then carried her from the room.

"What's on your mind?"

They lay in the semi-darkness together, she with her body curved into his, head resting in the crook of his arm as he held her hand against his chest.

"My mind is mush, after that," he joked. "I'm not as young as I used to be."

She craned her neck to look at him. "I haven't noticed any deterioration," she said, wryly. "Especially as you had a long day at work today."

Ryan let out a sigh and held her close as he recalled the events of the day. "I'm always reticent to tell you about it," he said. "I suppose I don't want to sully your mind with the things I've seen."

Anna squeezed his hand. "I knew what you did for a living from the moment we met," she said. "In fact, I seem to recall you being quite full of yourself—"

"Bravado," he chipped in. "I wasn't expecting to find you standing on my doorstep, and I had to say something rather than just stand there with my jaw on the floor."

She laughed. "I'll forgive you," she said. "But the point is, I'm not blind to the work you do; I'm proud of it, and of you. I admit, it isn't my chosen pathway, but that doesn't mean I'm too fragile to understand it, and share some of the load. I'm here, if you want to talk to me."

Ryan rubbed a hand along the smooth skin of her back.

"Thank you," he murmured. "Today was especially hard, but tomorrow will be harder again. I need to pay a visit to Gregson."

He felt her body tense, and was sorry for it. However, she had a right to know if there was a case that concerned any of the people formerly involved in The Circle, which had once counted her own father as its leader.

"Why?" she whispered.

"He may be connected to something we're investigating at the moment," he said, and then realised he needed to say more. "It's… concerning."

She was silent for a couple of beats, and then shifted so that she could look into his eyes.

"How concerning?"

"I don't know yet," he said, honestly. "We're dealing with a person, or perhaps several people, who've set up a scheme whereby individuals can nominate a person they'd like to have murdered by another member of the scheme, who will be a total stranger to them and the intended victim. As far as we can tell, the only stipulation is that, in exchange, they have to be prepared to kill somebody else's nominated victim, to whom they will be an equal stranger."

"So they all have alibis, and it's almost impossible for you to find a credible suspect?"

Ryan nodded. "As an added layer of protection, I think they try to make the deaths look like accidents or suicides," he said. "It's ingenious, if that's the right word for it."

Anna searched his face, and thought she saw fear hidden behind his eyes. "How big is this scheme?"

Ryan took her hand again, and held it. "I don't know the answer to that, yet, but I'm afraid that it will be huge. Another thing we don't know is how long it's been going on, or how far to extend our net. We're tugging at the very end of a thread, and we have no idea of knowing where it'll take us."

"And you think Gregson is behind it?"

"His name has come up, and, without wishing to blow smoke up his arse, the man has form when it comes to large-scale psychopathic murder rings."

"If he was bored, he could have just got an allotment," she said, and was pleased to see the flash of his smile.

"That would be too easy."

"Seriously, though. Why would he do this?"

"He's incarcerated for life," Ryan said quietly. "Arthur Gregson knows he's likely to die in prison, without any of the prestige, the money, the power that he worked so hard to achieve. He feels no remorse about any of the things he did; if he had his time again, he'd do the same things only taking care not to be caught out. He doesn't need money, or, at least, not much of it, because what's he going to do with it?"

"Drugs?" she wondered aloud.

"Maybe, but again, there's a ceiling on how many he can take in a day. In this case, I'm looking for someone who doesn't care about the money, which is why he or she doesn't charge for the service—as far as we know. Money isn't the primary objective."

"Gregson fits the bill, then."

Ryan nodded. "I'll know more, after tomorrow."

She reached up to cup his cheek, rubbing her hand against the light stubble she found there. "He's the one behind bars," she reminded him. "Arthur Gregson is an old, embittered man, but he only has words as his weapons, now."

Ryan thought of the words written in the classified ads, and shivered suddenly.

He tugged her against him again, brushing her lips with his own, breathing in the scent of her like a dying man. "I love you," he said again. He wanted her to know it, always.

She heard a note in his voice, something she couldn't place. "Hey," she whispered. "It'll be okay. You'll solve this—you always do."

"Do I?" he said, and wondered if there would ever come a time when he was faced with a problem he could never solve.

He'd seen enough of death to know that there were some things one simply could not fight.

"Go to sleep," he said softly, and kissed her hair.

CHAPTER 27

The next morning

"Daddy! Story, please!"

Ryan turned at the sound of his daughter's voice and moved away from the window, where he'd been watching the mist rolling across the valley. He cradled a cup of coffee in his hand, which he finished in a couple of gulps, and crouched down to meet Emma at her own height. She was dressed for nursery in a set of blue and pink dungarees, her dark hair arranged into two pigtails topped off with little blue bows, which suited her impish expression as she held out her preferred reading material.

"*Each Peach Pear Plum?*" he said. "An excellent choice."

He had only minutes left before he needed to leave for his interview at Frankland Prison, but he could always find time for Emma.

Arthur Gregson could wait.

The world could wait, so long as his daughter needed him.

"Come on, then," he said, and whisked her up onto the sofa in the conservatory, where she immediately snuggled herself into the crook of his arm and rested her head against his broad chest, where she could hear the strong, rhythmic beating of his heart.

"Each Peach—" he began.

"Pear Plum!" she finished for him, and then beamed a toothy grin.

Anna watched them from the kitchen, where she topped off her coffee and leaned back against the countertop. They were peas in a pod, she thought. Both were achingly beautiful, with minds as sharp as tacks…and both stubborn as the day is long. Her heart swelled as she listened to Ryan's voice while he read to their child, and she felt supremely grateful for all that life had gifted her. She had a small but loving family, which included Ryan's parents who treated her as another daughter, which was all the more poignant since they'd lost their own. Not forgetting their extended family, in the form of Frank, Denise, Jack and Mel, even Sandra Morrison and their friends further afield, such as Alex Gregory, who reminded her of the man Ryan might have been in the years before she'd met him. They had so much to be grateful for, but, as someone had once said, the more you gain, the more there is to lose…

"I have to get going."

She hadn't realised the story had finished, and Ryan stood before her with Emma cradled against his hip.

"Yes, I should too," she said, and pulled herself together. "I'll drop Emma at nursery. Before you go, I forgot to tell you, I went to view that house we were talking about in Bamburgh, yesterday."

Ryan's head was full of interview strategies and questions, but he set them aside to focus on that which was important to his family.

"And? What do you reckon?"

Anna couldn't hide her excitement. "The place needs updating, from top to bottom, but the potential is vast," she said. "I could imagine how it might look…"

"I knew it." Ryan smiled. "You loved that place the moment we stepped foot inside it, last year."

"Do you want to view it again, and remind yourself of how it looks?"

Ryan shook his head. "I trust you," he said. "Shall we put in an offer?"

"We haven't sold this place, yet!"

"I have a plan for that, remember?"

She smiled. "What if Frank and Denise don't go for it?"

"Then I'll throw his own words back in his face, and tell him he's a muppet."

"The Master of Persuasion strikes again."

Ryan laughed, and handed over their daughter, before kissing them both.

"Bye-bye, Daddy!"

He waved to her, but, as the front door shut behind him, Ryan felt another shiver, as though somebody had walked over his grave. He turned, desperate to go back inside, to where it was safe and warm, where he would be surrounded by those he loved most in the world.

But there were others who needed him.

He stepped away, and went in search of Death.

His Majesty's Prison Frankland was an uninspiring edifice on the outskirts of the city of Durham, built for purpose rather than for pleasure. Its utilitarian, red-bricked walls were home to a mixed bag of standard and high-risk male prisoners, which made for a volatile environment that wasn't helped by the dangerously low ratio of staff to prisoners, which was the same story throughout the prison service and was likely to remain so. As Ryan and Phillips knew, the general public wanted their retributive justice and the majority weren't interested in rehabilitation, especially amongst serious offenders; they wanted the security of knowing they were locked away behind bars without necessarily having to pay too much for it. Ryan could understand the sentiment, both as the surviving family member of a murder victim, and as a key part of the criminal justice system himself. On the other hand, as Phillips had rightly observed, he believed that people were capable of change.

Some of them, at least.

"How're you feelin'?"

Phillips asked the question as they passed through the first set of security gates, which opened with a loud *clank* of metal, and began making their way along a short corridor towards the next check point.

Ryan thought about giving some pithy remark about not having had enough caffeine, but there was no need to hide anything from Frank.

"I just want to get in there, get it over with, and get out again."

"You don't have to go in at all," Phillips said. "I don't mind givin' him the shakedown—"

Ryan shook his head. "It's always better to face the demon. Otherwise, they become more powerful in our imagination than in reality."

Phillips remembered that MacKenzie had said something similar when she'd decided to go and see Keir Edwards' body at the mortuary all those years ago. She told him that she needed to see her attacker dead, with her own eyes, so that he could die in her nightmares as well as in reality.

"Aye, that makes sense," he said. "If you change your mind, the offer stands."

They signed their names in the logbook, and began placing their belts, phones, wallets and other personal items inside trays for inspection. Once they were cleared, and were shown into a waiting area while an interview room was being prepared, Ryan turned to his friend with troubled eyes.

"Can I ask you something, Frank?"

"Anythin'," the other replied.

"I've never thought to say this before, but, now that Emma's here, and…and life has changed, it's been playing on my mind. I've asked my parents to be powers of attorney, if anything should ever happen to me, and they'd be wonderful grandparents to Emma; I know she'd want for nothing, either in love or in material things. But, when it comes to thinking about who we'd want to look after her, Anna and I have been meaning to ask you and Denise whether you would consider it."

Phillips was lost for words. "What—you mean, if anythin' was to happen to you, and—"

"If anything happens to me, then Anna would have Emma on her own, with support around her, I hope," Ryan said quietly. "But, if something was to happen to Anna *and* me, then Emma would need a family. My parents adore her, but they're not getting any younger. We admire you and Denise so much, and we see how you are with Samantha. We can't think of better people to bring Emma up, to love her and teach her the values we'd have wanted to teach her ourselves."

Phillips swallowed, hard. "I—I'm honoured you'd think of us," he said, huskily. "I know I can speak for Denise when I say we'd be only too glad to help, if the worst should happen."

"Good—"

Phillips put a firm hand on his friend's arm. "But, it *isn't* goin' to happen," he said, enunciating the word very clearly. "So there's no need to worry about it, is there?"

Ryan's smile didn't quite meet his eyes. "I don't know what's come over me, Frank. It's just—the past few days, I can't shake this feeling; the creeping sense that something bad is about to happen."

"In our business, that's normal," Phillips assured him, and gave him a pat on the back. "You need a holiday, that's all. Take a trip to that villa in Florence and soak up a few rays with a glass of vino tinto in your hand—that's the medicine."

"DCI Ryan? DS Phillips? We're ready for you now."

They nodded to the prison officer, who waited to take them along one of the long, white-washed corridors.

"Are you ready?" Phillips asked.

"I'm always ready," Ryan replied, and took the first step.

CHAPTER 28

Prison life had not been kind to Arthur Gregson, formerly Detective Chief Superintendent of the Northumbria Police Constabulary's Criminal Investigation Department. Despite having taken a criminal pathway in his later years, that couldn't remove his earlier career, and the many collars he'd taken during his stratospheric rise to the top of the ranks. There were people on the inside with scores to settle, and no amount of solitary confinement in the early years of his incarceration could have prevented the inevitable attacks that came unexpectedly, and on an almost monthly basis—until he found a way to protect himself. Gregson's body bore the marks of those early shivs, and, when he entered the room, their eyes were drawn to a long, jagged scar running down the length of his left cheek. However, he'd clearly made use of the prison gym—Gregson had always been tall and imposing, but now, he'd added a solid layer of muscle to his frame which was in stark contrast to the weathered skin of his face and the thin, close-cropped grey hair topping his head.

"Well, if it isn't my old *friends*," he said, genially. "Long time, no see."

"Take a seat, Arthur." Ryan offered no additional civility; once, he'd addressed this man as 'sir', and looked up to him as a mentor, but not anymore.

Never again.

If Gregson noticed, his face betrayed nothing of it and his manner remained polite, even *charming*; for all the world, as if he'd invited them there, for a cosy chat.

"You're looking tired," he said, and tutted. "Things keeping you busy at the moment?"

"What *things* might they be?" Ryan asked, before taking a seat at the metal table opposite him.

"You tell me," he said, eyes twinkling with excitement. "I've been rather out of the loop, lately, as you might imagine."

He still spoke in rounded tones, and they couldn't help but remember the times he'd walked along the corridors of Police Headquarters, his very presence an inspiration to young constables fresh out of the training academy and experienced officers alike.

He'd fallen far.

"It seems you have other interests, these days," Ryan said, not wishing to waste any time. "Fishing, for example?"

Gregson laughed and spread his hands. "I don't know if you've noticed, but there isn't much opportunity to cast a line from here," he said.

Phillips took out a printed copy of the subscriber list and showed him a highlighted entry. "Is that your name on this list?" he asked.

Gregson didn't bother to look at it. "Well, where's the harm? I like to learn about new things," he said. "It doesn't do to let yourself slide."

"Or to let your guard slip," Ryan murmured, and nodded towards the man's scar. "How'd that happen, Arthur?"

Gregson touched a finger to the old wound and shrugged. "A toothbrush, with two razor blades set into the plastic," he said, conversationally. "You might not know this, but it's much harder for the prison nurse to stitch the skin back together when there are two deep parallel cuts. I had to congratulate the bloke responsible, for his ingenuity if nothing else."

He'd also put his head through a door, at the first opportunity, but that was immaterial.

"How's my favourite redhead?" he asked, suddenly turning to Phillips. "I have to tell you, Frank, you're punching above your weight with Denise MacKenzie. What I wouldn't have given to have a crack at her—"

"We'll not speak of my wife, Arthur."

The words were spoken in a calm, level tone, but the meaning was explicit.

"Touchy, eh?" Gregson said, and laughed again. "Well, I can't say that I blame you. Must be hard, always playing second fiddle to this one." He jerked a thumb in Ryan's direction. "He's always the one the women notice, isn't he, Frank? Always the hero, the one in the papers, while you slog away as his sidekick, hoping for scraps. I don't know why you stand for it."

Ryan opened his mouth, but Phillips put a hand on his arm to stem the outburst.

"You'd know about playing second fiddle, wouldn't you, Arthur? Never the leader, always the led, that was you. Now, you're stitched up, in more ways than one." Phillips smiled. "What's the matter? Truth hurt?"

Gregson looked furious, then, in a flash, it was gone. "You're right about the fishing," he said. "I find it helps to have a hobby to pass the time, you know." He leaned forward, his eyes raking over the pair of them with unconcealed hatred. "In *fact*," he said, drawing the words out with relish. "I'm surprised to find we share something in common, Ryan. I never knew you were a keen fisherman."

Ryan frowned. "What do you mean?"

Gregson smiled slowly. "I suppose you haven't seen it yet," he said, in a voice dripping with sarcasm. "The latest edition of *The Northern Fisherman* came out this morning, and it makes for very interesting reading. You should pay particular attention to the 'Classified' section."

Without a word, Phillips took out his phone and began to call up the latest edition of the magazine, but Ryan had already seen the elation in Gregson's eyes which told him all he needed to know.

Beside him, he heard Phillips' sharp intake of breath.

"*Offered for sale*," Gregson whispered across the table. "*Several sets of fishing gear, free to good homes. Contact Maxwell Finley-Ryan, Elsdon, Northumberland. For collection ASAP and within two weeks, latest.*"

Ryan heard a humming in his ears, and black spots began to dance in front of his eyes.

"How does it feel?" Gregson snarled. "Eh? How does it *feel*?"

"What—what have you done?" Ryan said.

"You've done it," Gregson spat. "You've done it to yourself. You flew too high, Ryan, just like Icarus. You never know when to stop, and now your wings have melted away. The ground is rushing up to meet you and, before you know it, you'll be six feet under—"

Phillips threw back his chair then, and grabbed Gregson by the scruff of the neck.

"You evil *bastard*," he hissed. "I'll put your teeth down your throat—"

Gregson only laughed. "Still the loyal terrier, eh?" he said. "Go ahead, Frankie, and do your worst. It doesn't change a thing."

Ryan stood up, and swayed on his feet, the enormity of what lay before him crashing down.

"*Officer!*" Phillips called out urgently.

"Are you feeling all right, mate?" Gregson said, leaning back in his chair to enjoy the moment. "You look a bit peaky—"

"Shut your miserable mouth," Phillips growled, and put a strong arm around Ryan's waist. "C'mon, son. We're gettin' out of here—"

"Where are you gonna go, Ryan?" Gregson called back over his shoulder. "Where *can* you go?"

As a prison officer rushed inside, Ryan stumbled out into the corridor, stomach heaving.

"Steady, lad…steady."

Ryan braced his hands against the wall, sucking oxygen into his lungs until the sickness subsided.

"The advert names me, doesn't it?" he said, a part of him hoping Gregson had been wrong. "I have until the end of next week—that's right, isn't it?"

Phillips could only nod. "That's what it says. There's also somethin' about multiple sets, free to good homes. That's—"

Plural, Ryan thought. "It means several people have been assigned to the task of killing me," he said, softly. "All strangers to each other, and to me. I'll never see them coming."

"We—we'll get the whole of CID onto this," Phillips said, tremulously. "There's not a single person who wouldn't do all they can to help."

Ryan wasn't listening, because an even worse prospect had presented itself.

"Multiple sets could mean something else," he said. "It could mean my family, Frank. They might be under threat too."

Phillips couldn't argue with the possibility, and watched his friend rear back from the wall and pull out his smartphone to dial his wife's number with shaking fingers.

"What can I do?" he muttered. "Ryan? What can I do to help you?"

"Armed police," he said shortly. "We need an escort dispatched to the History Faculty, now—there's no answer, Frank. Anna's not answering."

He tried again, several times, without success.

"Don't panic, lad, stay calm—"

"There's no time, Frank. I'm going to get her myself."

"I'll come with you," Phillips said, hurrying to keep up with Ryan's long-legged strides. "I'll call the Firearms Unit on the way over. We're not far from the University."

Minutes, Ryan thought.

But it only took a few seconds to end a life.

They rushed through security, the bureaucracy of prison procedures eating into their precious time, until they emerged into the morning once more. The sun shone brightly, glinting against the barbed wire fencing and high-level cameras trained on every angle of the courtyard, but Ryan saw none of it as they hurried across the car park, his attention fixed entirely on securing the safety of his family.

"DCI Ryan! Wait!"

A voice called him back, and Ryan slowed down, angered by the interruption.

"Here! Chuck us the keys and I'll bring the car around!" Phillips called out to him, and Ryan nodded, hearing Frank's footsteps pounding the tarmac as he made his way in the other direction to meet the running figure who'd followed them out of the prison.

"Wh—"

"DCI Ryan! Your car! Stay away from the car! It's been t—"

They heard the explosion before they saw the mushroom of smoke and the lick of flames, which rose up into the sky with bang.

"*No,*" Ryan whispered, and then he was shouting, crying out his friend's name. "*Frank! FRANK!*"

Arms tried to hold him, but he shoved them off and sprinted towards the fire, legs screaming as he raced forward, eyes watering as smoke filled his vision.

Then, he saw him.

Phillips lay several metres clear of the blast area, his body outstretched as the force had thrown him backwards. The front of his coat was singed, and his trousers were aflame.

Ryan ran forwards, shrugging out of his coat before falling to his knees and using it to smother the flames.

"*Ambulance*! *We need an ambulance!*" he yelled, and one of the prison staff hurried to make the call.

Ryan's hands shook as he braced himself against the tarmac and leaned down to see if Phillips was still breathing.

No breath against his cheek.

He felt for a pulse against his friend's neck, a terrible silence blotting out all other sound as he waited to feel the comforting thud of a heartbeat.

Nothing.

"No," Ryan muttered. "No—no—"

Teeth gritted, he grasped the burnt embers of his friend's coat and pulled it open to reveal his shirt, which was also half-burnt. He found the spot beneath Phillips' breastbone, placed his hands over it, and began to pump, hard.

One…two…three…four…five…

He paused to breathe air into his friend's lungs, then began again.

One…two…three…stay with me, Frank…

He carried on, the muscles in his arms weeping with the effort, stopping after a minute or so to check for a pulse.

Still nothing.

"Again," Ryan muttered. "Again—"

Before he could continue, the medical officer from the prison arrived at the scene, armed with a defibrillator machine.

"No pulse," Ryan muttered. "Second attempt at CPR."

He didn't stop, but kept pumping his friend's heart while the medic rushed to prepare the machine that could jump-start it.

"Move out of the way," they said, and Ryan fell backwards to allow them to place the paddles on Phillips' chest. "CLEAR!"

Phillips' body shook, and Ryan waited, terror robbing the breath from his body.

Agonising seconds passed by.

"We've got a pulse," the medic said, and Ryan let out a sob of relief as he sat there on the tarmac beside him, letting the tears flow down his cheeks as he held the hand of a man who was, and would always be, the greatest friend he could have asked for.

He waited until the ambulance came to transfer Phillips to hospital and then, with a heavy heart, called MacKenzie, whose shock had been almost unbearable to hear.

But he could not join them, for there were others in danger.

There was no more time.

CHAPTER 29

It took less than ten minutes for a squad car to arrive outside the gates of Frankland Prison, alongside an armed police escort, who bundled Ryan into the car whilst their eyes scanned all around the car park. Then they were racing, sirens blaring through the quiet streets of Durham, never stopping until they reached the square outside Anna's faculty building. Students lounging on the grass looked across in surprise, passers-by stopped to stare as a tall, dark-haired man was ushered inside the hallowed walls of one of the country's premier centres for learning, alongside three firearms officers dressed in full combat gear.

Anna was mid-lecture when the doors at the top of the auditorium burst open to reveal her husband, and all heads turned to watch as he ran down the steps towards where she stood beside the lectern. Ryan heard their whispers and felt their eyes upon him, but saw only his wife—blessedly, still alive.

Her stomach did a funny sort of somersault when she saw the haunted look in his eyes, then the hard, focused expressions of the officers who manned the door, assault rifles in hand.

"Ryan, for God's sake, what's happened?"

"We have to leave, now," he said, and took her arm in a firm grip. "Please, Anna. Don't ask any questions."

"Wh—" Her feet stumbled to keep up, and tears threatened as she saw the faces of her students as they watched the spectacle, open-mouthed. "Emma? Is it Emma?"

Ryan shook his head, and hoped Jack and Charlie had retrieved her from nursery safely, by now. "She's being taken to Police Headquarters," he said. "That's where we're going, too."

"*Ryan!*" Her voice quivered as they crossed the foyer, and she was helped into the back of the squad car beside him. "What's *happening?*" She caught sight of blood on the cuffs of his shirt, and the smoky ash that clung to his skin and hair. "You're—you're bleeding—"

"It's not me," he said, and swallowed a fresh lump in his throat as he thought of his friend, who was, at that very moment, fighting for his life. "It was Frank."

Anna let out a strangled gasp.

"Car bomb," Ryan said, simply. "While we were inside Frankland speaking to Gregson, someone was outside, tampering with the car. They caught a figure on camera and tried to stop us, but Frank—he went ahead, to get the car started. I—Anna, I gave him the keys—" His breath hitched and fell as he battled tears.

"I don't understand—why?"

"There's a target on my head, Anna. They've put a call out to...I don't know how many people. It could be one, it could be twenty, but they all have the same objective, and that's to kill me."

She stared at him for endless seconds as the streets of Durham whipped by, and then tears began to fall in silent tracks down her face.

"What does it mean? What can we do?"

Ryan bore down against the urge to draw her in, because she could not join him in walking the road ahead and, if he weakened, he would not be able to let her go.

"You and Emma will be taken to my parent's home, Summersley, in Devon," he said. "You'll be there in under six hours."

"*No*," she said sharply. "I'm not going anywhere without you—"

He sucked in a breath, and then took her face in his hands, brushing away her tears with the pads of his thumbs.

"You have to trust me," he said. "I can't risk either of you, do you understand? The threat is real, Anna, and it's at our door. There isn't any room for error or for sentiment. This is the only way."

A sob escaped her lips, and she slumped forward into his waiting arms.

"Why can't—can't—you come—wi—with us?" she managed.

"Because it's me they're after," he said, stroking the soft fall of her hair. "You need to be far, far away, in order to be safe."

"But what about you?" she said, angrily. "What about *you*?"

A muscle ticked in his jaw. "I love you," he said. "I'll be doing all I can to come home to you.

I have people worth living for, worth fighting for, Anna."

She fell silent, but her tears seeped through the material of his shirt as they drove onward through the busy streets.

Sandra Morrison waited at the entrance of Police Headquarters, flanked by a line of officers.

"I want every available officer recalled," she said to the assistant, who hovered at her shoulder. "Cancel holidays, push off engagements…do whatever you have to do, but clear the diary. I want all the grunt work covered, so that our best men and women can focus their attention on what matters most."

"Which is?"

Morrison flicked a glance in her direction, then away again. "Family," she said simply.

Then, spotting the cavalcade of cars entering the car park, she walked forward to meet Ryan at the kerb. As he unfolded himself from the car, one look in his eyes might have reduced her to tears, if she'd let it.

"Ryan, Anna," she said, noting the other woman's sickly pallor and tear-streaked face with a heavy heart. "We have Emma with us, she's safe." She turned and began walking inside. "The moment I heard about Frank, we called in the Bomb Squad," she said brusquely. "They've swept the building and it's clear. We've stationed a guard on every exit, and the building is on High Alert. It's a fortress, as far as we can make it."

She saw that Ryan was already wearing a protective vest, but Anna hadn't yet been kitted out, so she barked out an order to remedy that immediately.

"Frank?" he asked, as they stepped inside the lift. "Have you heard any update about Frank?"

The doors shut, affording a few quiet moments as they travelled to the top floor.

"He's stable," she said. "He suffered a cardiac arrest, brought on by the shock of the blast, and a concussion as he fell backwards. They think a fracture to his collarbone, and first degree burns to his legs and chest—which could have been worse, if you hadn't intervened." She paused, and looked at him, as a mother might have done.

"It's because of your swift action that he's still with us at all, Ryan."

He looked away sharply, and waited until he could speak. "It's because of me that he was put in that position."

"Bollocks," she snapped at him, and both Ryans looked up in shock. "I won't stand for any of that talk. You can't predict the actions of some maniac, and you certainly aren't responsible for them."

The doors opened, and she moved off again, her footsteps drumming a staccato rhythm against the carpet tiled floor as she led them towards her own office at the far end of the corridor, where an armed guard stood outside the door.

When they opened it, they were greeted by the sound of a child's laughter, and saw Emma seated on the floor beside Charlie Reed, who was teaching her to play snakes and ladders.

"Don't think this means I'm opening a creche in the office," Morrison said, and cleared the obstruction in her throat. "Go and see your daughter, Ryan."

While Anna rushed forward, he paused to look at the woman beside him.

"Thank you, ma'am."

Morrison shook her head, at a loss. "I want them on the road within twenty minutes," she said. "Where are you sending them?"

Ryan looked across at his wife and daughter. "To the only person I'd trust with their lives," he replied. "I'm sending them to my father."

She nodded.

"Have you found a driver?" he asked her.

"I didn't have to," she replied. "Lowerson volunteered immediately."

Ryan looked across at the man who stood guard at the window, watching the car park below. He couldn't have wished for a better envoy, and wished he had the words to express his gratitude.

Morrison put a hand on his shoulder, then left him to enjoy a few minutes with his family before they were parted.

CHAPTER 30

It had been said before that parting was a sweet sorrow but, on that day, there was only sorrow.

Emma's arms clung to his neck as Ryan settled her in a car seat in the back of an unmarked police car, and he spoke softly to her, knowing that her young mind couldn't fail to comprehend that something was badly wrong.

He leaned in, and brushed a kiss on her smooth forehead.

"Emma? Listen to me, now—"

"*No!*" she screamed, growing red in the face. "I want to go home! I want Daddy!"

His heart shattered, but his voice never wavered. "Listen, sweetheart," he repeated, and her lip quivered. "You're going on an adventure to see Grandma and Grandad, in Devon."

She looked up at him with big, trusting eyes. "Grandie?" she repeated.

She loved her grandfather.

"Mm hmm," Ryan said. "Mummy's going with you, and Uncle Jack's going to do the driving. Now, I've got to stay here for a while and do some important work—"

"To help people," she said, and he nodded.

"That's right," he said, and stroked a gentle hand over her head. "You can read to Grandma and Grandad, and explore the gardens. They've got a new puppy, too, you know."

"Really?" she said. "A *puppy*?"

Ryan smiled. "A golden Labrador," he said. "He might need some company, don't you think?"

Emma nodded, and settled back in her seat.

"I'll see you soon," he said, and hoped it was true. "Look after Mummy, and be a good girl, all right?"

She nodded, and puckered up for a kiss.

"Love you, Daddy."

"I love you too, little one."

He kissed her goodbye, and then straightened up, fighting a rising tide of emotion. Anna stood on the other side of the vehicle, hair blowing in the afternoon breeze as she waited for him.

In that moment, he thought she'd never been more beautiful.

Ryan walked around to take her in his arms, kissing her hair, her face, then her mouth, cradling her face in his hands.

Then, he set her away, when she would have held on for longer.

"No," he said softly. "It's time to go. I love you, Anna."

"I love you too," she said, choking back tears. "Please, be careful."

"I will."

Ryan held open the car door for her, and waited until she was strapped inside before turning to Lowerson, who stood to one side.

"Don't stop unless you have to," he said. "They're expecting you, at the other end."

Jack nodded, and moved towards the car. Before he could, Ryan pulled him in for a hard hug.

"Thank you," he muttered. "I won't ever forget this, Jack."

Lowerson looked up at his friend, the man who'd always believed in him, even when he'd lost himself along the way.

"It's an honour," he said gruffly. "And the very least I can do."

He stepped aside, and settled himself in the driver's seat.

"Drive like the wind," Ryan murmured, raising a hand to wave at his wife and daughter.

Lowerson nodded and, a moment later, the car pulled away, taking everything that was most precious with it.

CHAPTER 31

Charles Ryan stood in the large, panelled library of his home in Devonshire and looked out across the formal gardens. They spread for a quarter of a mile before reaching the lake, across from which there was a beautiful crypt in the style of a Grecian folly, trailing with ivy and honeysuckle, where his daughter, Natalie, was buried. Most days, he liked to take a walk down there and feed the ducks, then sit quietly on the bench beside the crypt, which was his favourite place to think.

He hadn't fed the ducks today, nor taken his usual walk.

When his wife entered the room, she thought that it could have been her son standing there by the window. At well over six feet, they shared the same height and athletic build, the same upright posture and air of command which eluded many people but was ingrained into every fibre of their being. From behind, they were almost identical, were it not for the colour of their hair.

"Anna's on the road now," she said quietly. "Jack Lowerson's driving her and little Emma down. They should be with us in a few hours."

Charles looked down at his watch, then across at his wife, whose lovely face was marred by worry.

"I've alerted the security team," he said. "They're on their way, and, in the meantime, I've got our men here on standby. They're all trained specialists, as you know."

In addition to being adept at land management, his team of groundsmen were also handy with a rifle. It helped that several had been members of his security attachment in the old days, when Charles travelled the world working in British intelligence, then as one of Her Majesty's diplomats and, later, as an ambassador. Life was much quieter now that he was retired, but his former career enabled him to call in a few favours, when the occasion demanded it.

"I wish they'd let me arrange a flight for them," he muttered.

"No time," she said. "Perhaps it's safer this way." She pressed her lips together, and crossed the room to stand beside him. "I'm worried, Charles."

Eve Finley-Ryan was not a woman given to panic; she'd lived through enough emergencies in their shared lifetime to become as desensitized to them as he was. However, she was a mother above all else, and it was that protective instinct which had led them to send Max and his sister, Natalie, away to boarding schools, so that they would be safely housed and cared for while they were at work, abroad—sometimes in war-torn countries. It was a decision Charles had lived to regret, for it created an irreparable separation between him and his son, but he could not turn back the hand of time. He could only hope that, over the past few years, he'd gone some way towards making amends with his only remaining child, of whom he was fiercely proud.

He looked out across the lawn and smiled, remembering two dark-haired children playing 'tag' amongst the ornamental hedgerows; a boy and a girl who'd laughed together. Now, one of them was consigned to his memory, while the other was under threat of joining his sister in the same marble tomb across the water from where they stood.

He would not allow that to happen.

"I'm worried as well," Charles said. "I can't let him face this alone, and I won't."

Eve nodded, and knew what he was going to say without him needing to speak the words aloud. "When are you going?"

He stuck his hands in the pockets of his chino trousers, and the action reminded her of the young man she'd fallen in love with, all those years before.

"As soon as Anna arrives with Emma," he said. "I'll travel back up north with their driver."

"Is Ryan expecting you?"

Charles shook his head. "If I tell him, he'll try to put me off," he said, and smiled at the thought. "I don't want to have to pull rank but, when it comes to situations such as these, his father does know best."

Eve took his hand, and he tugged her close.

"I've spoken with my contacts in GCHQ," he continued, pressing a kiss to her temple. "I've pulled every string I can, but none of them can give us anything we don't already know. It'll take days to try to trace the IP address of the person placing the ads in that magazine—maybe longer."

She tried to follow the lessons she'd been taught since she was Emma's age, about how to repress her fear and present a calm front, to build a wall behind which she could hide her true feelings, but that woman no longer existed.

"I can't lose both of them," she whispered, and let out a ragged sob. "I can't, Charles…I couldn't live through that pain again. *Please*. Please make sure he doesn't come to harm—"

He held her in his arms while she wept, and thought of the day his son had been born, almost forty years earlier. He remembered the fear he'd felt as he'd cradled the baby in his arms, wondering how he, Charles Ryan, could have helped to create something so perfect. The enormity of the responsibility had been overwhelming, but then Max had opened his eyes and looked up at him with absolute trust. There had been no fear then, only a deep and abiding desire to protect the tiny bundle from harm.

The feeling hadn't changed, even if the bundle was now as tall as he was.

I'm an older man, Charles thought to himself. No longer as sprightly as he might once have been, and the muscles he worked hard to maintain were nothing in comparison with their strength, once upon a time. But he could still shoot a moving target a hundred yards away, and he could take down a lesser man in close combat through willpower and training alone, if need be. Beyond this, he was a strategist, a born leader, and a concerned father.

"I won't let him come to harm, Eve. You have my word. I'd sooner die than lose another one of our children."

She looked out across the gardens, where one of their men patrolled the far lawn, a rifle slung over his shoulder. "Why?" she wondered aloud. "Why does Ryan do it?"

"His work?" Charles said. "He does that which others aren't able to, because it's necessary. Without people like him, the world would be a much darker place, Eve. He's a bastion of all that's good; all that's worth protecting."

Eve rested her head against his shoulder. "I wonder where he got it from," she said.

"No," he said, in a voice thick with emotion. "Ryan isn't like me. He's a far better man than I ever was."

She squeezed his hand. "Why don't we take a walk and feed the ducks?"

He nodded, and raised her fingers to his lips. "That sounds like a good idea—"

"Charles, what if they all came and lived here, with us?" Eve said, a bit desperately. "Ryan, Anna and Emma could come and stay. We could protect them, and, God knows, he has no real need to work...he could help you manage the estate, and—and—" Her eyes filled with tears, and her voice trailed away.

"And it would be like caging a bird," he finished for her. "A gilded cage, perhaps, but still a cage. We can't hide him away from the world, nor ourselves, as much as we might like to, sometimes. We have to face it, live it and, yes, sometimes just *survive* it. Ryan knows that, which is why he's chosen to stay up there. It's the most sensible, selfless action to take, because it removes his wife and child from the threat of harm."

Eve knew he was right, but — "I just love him so much."

As do I, he thought. *As do I.* "Come on," he said quietly, linking his fingers through hers. "Let's go and sit beside Natalie, and enjoy the sunshine while we can."

CHAPTER 32

Hundreds of miles further north, Ryan made his way back inside Police Headquarters to find that a task force had already been set up, with Morrison at the helm. The main conference room was full to brimming with police personnel, many of whom had given up their free time to offer their service to a man who had consistently gone above and beyond, or shown kindness to them in ways too innumerable to mention. This was the case for Charlie Reed, who had already arranged for childcare over the next few days, so that she might offer her undivided support to Ryan, who was not only her new boss but a symbol of why she had chosen to enter law enforcement in the first place.

As he entered the room, conversations stopped, and chairs were pushed back as able-bodied men and woman came to their feet.

Ryan looked around the faces of his friends and colleagues. "I just want to thank you," he said. "I'm sorry, I can't think of much more than that. Just…thank you."

The clapping began, softly at first, then building to a crescendo as more hands joined in to express their solidarity.

"Sir?"

He looked around, eyes bright with unshed tears, to find one of the PCs standing there with a cup of hot coffee and a bacon sandwich.

"From Detective Sergeant Phillips," she explained, with a shy smile. "We received a message from him, a few minutes ago, via DI MacKenzie. He says you're to eat this to keep your strength up, and keep your chin up, too."

She turned away, then clicked a finger. "Oh—he also said to pass on the message that, just because he wasn't very responsive while you gave him the kiss of life, you're not to take it to heart. He doesn't think you're a bad kisser, but he'll give you a few pointers in that direction once he's back in the office."

Ryan's eyes crinkled at the corners, and a slow smile spread over his face. "Understood," he said softly. "Thank you, constable."

He moved across to the front of the room, where Morrison was in the process of marking up a timeline on the whiteboard.

"Been a while since I've done this," she said, without looking at him. "It's like riding a bike, isn't it?"

Ryan didn't feel especially hungry but, with Frank's words ringing in his ears, he lifted the sandwich to his lips and took a healthy bite. "I don't expect you to do this," he said, after a minute. "You must have far more important—"

She turned on him, unexpectedly angry. "Don't you dare finish that sentence," she warned him. "After all these years, and all the cases we've been through together, don't insult me by suggesting that I would do any less for my—my friend." She cleared her throat. "You might be a royal pain in the arse, Ryan, but your *ours*."

Denise MacKenzie had much the same thought as she took a seat in one of the plastic-coated visitors chairs next to her husband's bed in the Royal Victoria Infirmary. He was, according to the nurses on the ward, one of their most difficult patients; not, they hastened to add, because he was anything less than charming, but because it required constant vigilance to ensure he followed their instructions and rested himself. Even now, she could tell by the look on his grumpy face that he resented being stuck in a hospital bed, hooked up to wires and machines, when he'd rather be out in the field, helping his friend.

"Stop fiddling with that bandage," she said, sternly.

Phillips drummed his fingers against the bedsheets and glowered at her.

"I was only adjustin' it," he argued. "I don't need all these bloody things, anyhow. I'm absolutely *fine*—"

"You had a cardiac arrest," she said. "Brought on by the shock."

"Well, you'd have jumped out of your own skin if a car bomb went off in your face, wouldn't you?"

"Maybe I would, but we're not talking about me, Frank."

"Semantics," he muttered, and she heard the regular *beep* of his ECG monitor begin to sound faster, indicating a rise in heart rate.

She rose to her feet and came to perch carefully on the edge of the bed.

"Frank, listen to me," she said, and leaned over to kiss the tip of his nose. "I know how strong you are, and how frustrating it must be for you to be stuck in here, but there's no way you're leaving this room until the doctor gives you the 'all clear'. Is that understood?"

MacKenzie was a wonderful woman at the best of times, he thought. But when she was ticking him off like Nurse Nightingale? Then, she was magnificent.

His heart rate spiked again, as he gazed into her eyes.

"Frank?"

"Yes, my angel?"

"Don't even think about it."

"Wha—howay, man! You can't blame a guy for dreamin', can you?"

"I can, if his thoughts are so spicy he's liable to bring on another cardiac incident," she said. "Now, just settle down and eat your jelly."

She shook her head, and brushed the hair back from his brow.

"Frank?"

"Yes, love?"

"Scare me like that again, and I'll kill you myself."

"Yes, Nurse."

"Oh, you—"

Uncaring of the bandages, or of the throbbing pain in his head, he tugged her towards him and stole a kiss from her outraged lips.

"You're a menace," she muttered, after she'd administered his favourite kind of medicine.

"Aye, it's often been said. How's our lad?" he asked.

"Ryan's being looked after," she said, and gave his hand a squeeze. "Morrison has rallied the entire department around, so you don't have to worry."

But he did.

"What about Anna and Emma? The girls—"

"They're already on their way to Devon," she said. "You need to relax now, and concentrate on getting better. You've got your own girls to think about."

His eyes filled with sudden tears.

"I don't want Samantha to know about this," he said, quite seriously. "She's had enough loss and grief in her life, without having to worry about me, too."

Denise started to object.

"Why not say I've been called away with work, and will be home in a few days?"

"I don't want to lie to her, Frank."

He sighed, because he didn't want to, either. "In that case, just tell her I'll be home soon."

She thought about it, and then gave a brief nod. "I'll do that. Rest now, Frank."

"Oh no—"

His heart rate increased once more, and she jumped up.

"What's the matter? Should I call for the nurse?"

"No, no," he muttered, and folded his arms across his bandaged chest. "I was just thinkin', I'll have to rearrange the Dance-Off. I tell you, that Melissa's got off on a reprieve—"

If there hadn't been another patient on the ward, Denise might cheerfully have murdered him, then and there.

"Ryan?"

He looked up from his inspection of a list of cold cases, to find Charlie Reed hovering beside him.

"Charlie? Have you found something?"

She pulled up a chair beside him, and laid a file on the desk. "Maria Dawson, died two years ago in a drowning accident at Dunstanburgh," she said, without preamble. "The case was reported locally, but it was passed off as a bad accident. According to the report, she was standing too close to the edge of the cliff, down by Egyncleugh Tower, and was found washed up in Queen Margaret's Cove which is directly beneath." She referred to a rocky inlet to the east of Dunstanburgh Castle, rumoured to have been named after Margaret of Anjou.

"According to Frank, 'Egyncleugh' means 'Eagle's Ravine' in Northumbrian dialect," Ryan muttered.

"Sorry?"

"Never mind," he said, and made a grab for the file. "I suppose Maria Dawson is the late wife of John, the Club Secretary?"

"Yes," she said. "He was away on a golfing trip in St Andrew's at the time she died."

"Of course he was," Ryan said.

"He must have been the one who killed Harding," Charlie said. "There's no other plausible explanation for it. He had the means and opportunity—and, now, we know he had a motive, of sorts. The problem is a lack of forensic evidence."

Ryan flicked through the pages of the file, then snapped it shut again. "There's enough to bring him in for questioning," Ryan said. "We'll see how confident he is once he's been sitting in an interview room stewing in his own juices for half an hour. Contact Waddell and tell him to bring him in."

Reed nodded. "About Kath Hopkins," she said. "I hope you don't mind, but I took the initiative and had Duncan Fraser's mountain bike seized and brought in for forensic testing—"

"Charlie, that's exactly the kind of initiative I like to see. In fact, I should have done it myself."

"You've been busy," she reminded him, with a smile. "Well, as you can imagine, Faulkner's pulled out all the stops and has been calling the lab almost every hour. They've just come back to confirm that they've detected minute traces of the white powder we found inside the Range Rover on the handlebars of the bike."

Ryan smiled. "If Fraser's story about the car having been stolen was true, and he had absolutely nothing to do with Hopkins' murder, there's no possible way in which that powder could have found its way onto the handlebars. Bring him in, too—under arrest on suspicion of murder."

Charlie nodded. "The Bomb Squad are going over the remains your car, now," she said. "I'll let you know if they find anything useful."

Ryan looked at the time on the wall, then at the young woman who stood ready and able to keep going, keep helping, until she dropped.

"It's after four; why don't you go and see your little boy now, Charlie."

"No, I—"

"It wasn't a question, Reed. It was an order."

Spoken kindly, and with a smile.

"I'm happy to stay on here," she argued.

"I know, and I'm grateful to you. Go home to your son, and do what I can't do, at the moment; hold your child close, watch cartoons, eat fish fingers."

She gave him a lop-sided smile. "All right," she said. "Before I go, have you—ah—have you heard anything from Jack?"

"They've just arrived in Devon," he said, and watched relief pass over her face. "He said all went smoothly, aside from the hundreds of rounds of 'I Spy' Emma subjected him to, on the journey down."

Still, she lingered. "Are you going to be all right, sir?"

Ryan gave her a lop-sided smile. "I always am," he said.

It was only later that she realised he hadn't answered her question.

CHAPTER 33

Charles Ryan held out a scrap of bread to his granddaughter, who clutched it in her little fist and then lobbed it neatly into the lake, where a gaggle of ducks hurried over to eat it, despite having downed the best part of a loaf only a few hours earlier.

"They're hungry!" she cried out.

"They certainly are," he said, and swung her up onto his shoulders. "Shall I show you where your daddy liked to play, when he was a little boy?"

"Yes please, Grandad!"

He began walking towards the edge of the lawn, beyond which was a forested area where Ryan had built his dens and where, one magical summer, Charles had built him a treehouse fit for a prince. The wood had weathered over the years, and parts had been replaced for safety, but he'd never had the heart to tear it down, so there it remained, a testament to a time when father and son had camped amongst the trees and looked up at the stars together.

As if she'd read his mind, Emma began to sing 'Twinkle, Twinkle' at the top of her voice, and, to his surprise, he found himself singing along. Presently, they dipped beneath the canopy and he put her back on her feet, so she could trudge over the undergrowth beside him until they came to a clearing, of sorts, encircled by six or seven large trees, their trunks thick and gnarled with age. Rope bridges hung between them, connecting one to the other, while miniature huts had been built like milecastles on each tree, with a larger construction spanning two levels on the largest of all.

"*Look*, Grandad! *Look*!"

He smiled, and caught her up in his arms so that she could see things better.

"Is that Daddy's treehouse?" she asked.

"He shared it with his sister, your Auntie Natalie, who died before you were born, darling."

"Can I play in it?"

"Of course," he said, and kissed her cheek. "It's yours, now, to explore, so long as one of us is holding your hand."

"Grandad?"

"Yes, sweetheart?"

"Are you scared of falling?"

Charles ran a hand over her head, and smiled. "If I was scared, I'd never have built this treehouse," he said. "But it's okay to be scared sometimes, Emma."

Charles returned with Emma on his shoulders half an hour later, and Eve watched them crossing the lawn from the kitchen window, with Anna by her side.

"I wish Ryan could see this," Eve whispered.

Anna turned to her mother-in-law and put a comforting arm around her waist. "He'll come and visit next time," she said, with more confidence than she was feeling. "We'll all go for a walk together."

Eve turned to Lowerson, who was sitting at the enormous old kitchen table enjoying her hospitality.

"How are those scones, Jack?"

"Delicious, Mrs Ryan, thank you."

"Can I offer you anything else, dear?"

"I don't think I could manage it, even if I wanted to," he said, with a smile and a yawn. "I'd better be getting on the road, soon."

"You're welcome to stay overnight," she offered.

He shook his head. "Thank you, but no. I need to get back."

Anna wished she was going with him, and turned away to look out of the window again, eyes blurring with tears. "Tell Ryan I miss him," she said huskily.

Eve rubbed a hand over her daughter-in-law's back but, before she could say anything further, Emma ran inside looking rosy-cheeked.

"Grandma! Mummy! Uncle Jack! There's a giant treehouse in the garden! It's the biggest thing I've ever seen!"

Anna smiled and scooped her up for a hug. "Is it, now?"

"Ah-ha, and Grandpa says he'll turn it into a castle for me, if I want!"

Charles joined them, having kicked off his wellies in the boot room outside.

"A castle fit for a princess," he said, with a wink. "Why don't you do a drawing of what you'd like, and I'll see if I can build it for you?"

Emma wriggled out of her mother's arms and hurried off to the little play desk in the corner, where they kept a pot of crayons and some paper for grand designs such as these.

"Time to get going," Charles said to Jack, who nodded and left them to make their farewells. "Anna?"

She found herself enveloped in a hug.

"Take care of yourself, and our little princess," he said. "This will all be over, soon."

Anna could find no words, so she simply nodded.

"Eve?"

His wife drew herself together, and tried to smile. "Be careful," she told him.

Charles kissed her, blew one for his granddaughter, and then was gone.

Darkness had fallen by the time Ryan emerged from the Interview Suite, where he and Sandra

Morrison had spent an exhausting few hours trying to draw out Duncan Fraser and John Dawson, without much success. No matter which way they'd questioned them, neither man had budged an inch from their 'no comment' answers, which could be another stipulation of their membership in the killing scheme.

"We'll keep them in here, overnight," Morrison said, rubbing her tired eyes. "Maybe that'll loosen their tongues."

"They're stubborn, I'll give them that," Ryan said. "Neither of them blinked at the mention of *The Northern Fisherman,* either. They were expecting it."

They made their way back upstairs to where the task force still worked, although at a less frantic pace than before.

"It's time everyone went home," Ryan said. "It isn't that I don't appreciate the effort, because I do, but we're not going to make progress until we find out who's behind those adverts, and that relies on digital forensics. Pulteney has handed over all of his electronics—voluntarily, I might add—so it seems unlikely he's the one behind it all, but you never know. Gregson remains a possibility, so we can look at him again tomorrow."

"It may be that Gregson placed the advert without being the mastermind behind it all," Morrison said.

"That's also possible," he agreed. "The real question to ask myself is: who hates me enough to want me dead?"

"It may not be personal," Morrison reminded him. "This could be a transactional motivation, where they want to remove you in order to prevent you from making a discovery."

"Others could still do that," he said. "Charlie, Jack…any one of you could crack it. Killing me doesn't stop that from happening."

Morrison nodded and, after dismissing the staff to their homes and beds, she picked up the conversation again. "I've authorised round-the-clock armed support," she said, and held up a hand when he would have argued. "I don't *care* what it costs the department, before you ask. I can get you into a safe house for tonight, and however long you need."

Ryan thought of his home, and its unique position.

Then, he thought of what he and Phillips had discussed the other day, about fear and facing one's demons.

"If I go into hiding, I'll never come out," he said. "They'll only wait for me to emerge again. I'd rather stay in my own home, with some additional security."

She considered the idea, and then nodded. "I'll send a couple of specialists over to sweep the place, first," she said. "You can have my spare room this evening, and go home tomorrow morning with an armed guard."

Ryan raised an eyebrow. "Your spare room?"

"*Yes*," she said. "I want you where I can keep an eye on you. Between you and Frank, I've lost years off my life in stress today, and I've no intention of losing any more. I'm not getting any younger, as it is." She pointed a finger at him. "You don't snore, do you? The walls are thin in my house."

Ryan blinked. "I've no idea. Anna hasn't mentioned anything about it."

"Well, that doesn't tell me very much," Morrison laughed. "Your wife loves you so much, she'd probably put up with you snoring like a wart hog."

It was quite an image.

"Give her a call," Morrison advised. "Tell her you're okay, and then we'll get moving. You can ask her about the snoring while you're on."

"Yes, ma'am."

CHAPTER 34

The next morning

The village of Elsdon still slept while a dark green land vehicle crawled through its main street, the driver a shadowed figure behind the wheel. The dawn was breaking as he parked on the outskirts of the village, in a lay-by near to a monument known as 'Winter's Gibbet', where a man was hanged in 1791 and from which a prosthetic head still hung as a grisly reminder of what used to be the penalty for those who committed murder.

Ignoring it, he avoided the roads and made his way over the moorland on foot, stopping first to retrieve a rifle from the passenger side of his car. The man was sure-footed on the rough terrain, and had no need of a map; he would have known the direction to take even with his eyes closed. Thin rays of light spread out across the valley, which came to life in shades of blue and green to create a perfect Arcadian scene as he walked, keeping tightly to the hedgerows. Soon, he passed a smart equestrian facility, and knew he'd almost reached his destination.

He'd brought provisions, in case the wait was a long one, but he was reliably informed that Ryan would be back in his own home that very morning, and there would never be a better time to catch him and his team of firearms specialists off-guard. A recce the previous day had elicited a few good spots with a clear view of the patio, with its enormous glass windows, and, so long as he was patient, the perfect moment would eventually present itself.

He decided on a comfortable spot to the west of Ryan's property, which had an elevated position and was also shielded by a line of trees, for cover. He moved into position and took his time checking the sight on his rifle, only to be surprised by the sound of a car's engine making its way up the narrow hill towards the house.

Earlier than expected, he thought, and crouched beside a tree to watch the car's progress through the gaps in the hedgerow, where Ryan often ran in the mornings, according to the research dossier. The driveway and front door were around the other side of the property, where he had no line of sight, but he raised his rifle in anticipation of Ryan's arrival into his kitchen area. From there, he only needed him to move to the window, just once, and look out across the pretty hillside.

Minutes passed by, and he saw figures moving within the house but there was no clear shot. His frustration began to rise in line with the cortisol in his body, while sweat beaded on his forehead and ran down the back of his neck.

"Come on," he muttered. "*Come on.*"

He experienced a moment's doubt, and reminded himself of the reason why he was doing this. There was a debt to pay, and, after all, he'd been given his greatest wish, which had allowed him to prosper and live as he desired. It was only fair that he returned the favour for somebody else. Part of him wondered about the man's family and whether he had any children, then he shoved the thought aside and re-focused his attention on the patio doors.

Don't humanise the victim, he'd been told.

His finger hovered over the trigger, shaking slightly in anticipation of the kill.

Then, his chance came.

Even at that distance Ryan was unmistakeable, with his tall, broad-shouldered body and handsome features and, just for a moment, he experienced a funny sort of guilt; as though he was on the cusp of murdering something much bigger than a man, and more meaningful.

A superman.

He shook himself, and, before he could think about it any longer, aimed the rifle and pulled the trigger.

A single gunshot rang out into the quiet morning, sending birds squawking into the sky. In the distance, he heard the sound of glass shattering and, raising his field glasses, he saw that Ryan was no longer standing, but had fallen to the floor where he lay, unmoving.

Superman was only human, after all.

EPILOGUE

One week later

*The Assembly Rooms,
Newcastle upon Tyne*

Chief Constable Morrison smoothed down her dress uniform and made her way up to the front of a staged area, where a lectern stood beside a large, black-and-white image of Detective Chief Inspector Maxwell Finley-Ryan, flanked by an enormous display of cream and white roses. She held a sheet of paper in her hand containing a speech she'd prepared for the occasion but, as she looked out across the sea of men and women in uniform, she found she didn't need it, after all.

"There are many things I could say about our late friend and colleague, DCI Ryan," she began, working to keep the tremble from her voice. "I could tell you about all the times he ignored my advice or flouted protocols in order to get his man. I could tell you of the numerous occasions on which he bent the rules, but I wouldn't want to give the newbies amongst you any ideas."

There was a fluttering of polite laughter.

"I could speak of my admiration for his integrity, his heart, his work ethic or the loyalty he showed to his friends and colleagues here, but I'm not going to, because there's someone far better qualified to do that. I'd like to invite his closest friend, Detective Sergeant Frank Phillips, to share some of his memories with us all, instead."

Phillips, who was seated on the front row, took a moment to compose himself, and then stood up and walked slowly and carefully to the stage. He waved away the offer of a chair, and braced his hands on the lectern, wondering where to begin.

"I remember the first day I met Maxwell Ryan," he said, looking out among the faces of those he recognised, and many he didn't. "My first thought was that he was far too good lookin', and that he'd probably be a reet poser."

There was another rumble of laughter.

"But, you know, as I got to know the lad, I realised he was the last one to think of how he looked, because he was far more interested in other things…like helpin' people. That was his favourite hobby, come to think of it. Whether it was trackin' down killers or lendin' someone a few bob, he was the first to put his hand in his pocket. He'd have given you his last fiver, if he thought you needed it."

There were rumbles of agreement around the company, from those like Tom Faulkner, who'd received help from Ryan in years gone by to clear a crippling debt, to those such as the office cleaning team, who were never forgotten, and always received a small envelope to supplement their pay each Christmas.

"He always went above and beyond because he *cared* for people. He dealt with some of the worst, but he still managed to like people, and want the best for them. I should know, because I was lucky enough to call him my friend—"

Phillips' voice broke, and he stopped for a moment, gathering his strength to continue.

"He was often kind enough to say that he'd learned from me, but, what he didn't realise was how much I learned from *him*," he continued. "If I was a good man, it's because I was inspired to be. If I was a good detective, it's because I had a better one standing beside me, to spur me on. We are only the sum total of the people who grace our lives, and I'll be forever grateful that he graced mine."

A tear escaped, and he brushed it away.

"He wasn't a believer, so I won't say he's in a better place, behind a set of pearly gates. I'll just say, 'Here's to you, son, wherever you may be.' You're missed by all of us, and will never be forgotten."

Phillips stepped away, and MacKenzie was the first to stand and clap, before hundreds followed her example and rose to their feet to honour a man they thought would live forever.

Summersley, Devon

The same day

The service was a small one, attended only by Ryan's close family.

The sun shone brightly that day, casting its gentle rays over the white marble mausoleum as they gathered inside to lay another of their number to rest beside Natalie. The interior was not the stuff of nightmares, but an architectural feat with a large stained-glass cupola in its domed ceiling which spread multicoloured light across the marble tombs within.

"He's where he would have wanted to be," Eve whispered. "Beside Natalie."

Anna bore down against a fresh wave of tears and reached for her mother-in-law's hand, holding it tightly in her own.

"It should have been me," Ryan said, quietly.

Eve turned to her son, who stood on her other side, stricken with grief. He wore a dark suit, borrowed from his father's wardrobe, and, with the sun at his back, it could have been Charles standing there beside her, the man she'd met on another sunny day, in London.

She reached across and took his hand, so the three of them were joined.

"There isn't any other way he would have chosen to leave this world, than in the course of protecting his family," his mother said, and knew that to be the absolute truth. "He was so proud of you."

Ryan's tears fell like rain, and he turned, striding outside into the open air, where he stood looking out across the lake.

Anna left Eve to be with Charles and followed Ryan outside, standing back to allow him space to grieve in solitude until she sensed that he would want her company. Then, she crossed the lawn to join him beside the water.

"I'd known him my whole life," Ryan said. "But, still, I felt I hardly knew him at all."

Anna understood what he meant. "We always wish there was more time," she said. "Even just one more day."

She'd lost all of her family, the good and the bad, and would have given all she owned for just one more hour with her mother.

"I never told him how much I loved him."

"He knew," Anna said, without any shadow of a doubt. "Charles knew that."

Up ahead, an enormous mansion, white painted and bathed in sunlight, shone like a beacon in the centre of many acres of land. For generations, it had been home to the Ryan family, passing from father to son along with an honorary title that none of them ever used.

"What now?" Anna asked.

Ryan ran a hand through his hair, and let it fall away again. "The estate is managed very well by an existing team," he said quietly. "As far as I'm concerned, this is my mother's house, certainly not mine, therefore it will be her decision what she would like to do with it."

"She wouldn't want to leave Natalie and your father behind," Anna said, and he nodded his agreement.

"On the other hand, it's a big place, and it's easy to be lonely," he said.

"We can keep her company for a while, to help with any arrangements or just to be there while she goes through the worst of the grief, if she'd like?"

"I was hoping you'd say that," he said. "Besides, the investigation is still ongoing in the North. They've arrested several killers, and they're continuing to uncover more every day, but Atherton's murderer hasn't been found and they haven't identified the person who planted the bomb on my car, either."

He frowned, thinking of a landscape far removed from the gentle countryside where they now stood.

"I have the impression of a spider in the centre of a web," he said slowly. "We're unravelling the web, but we've yet to find the spider."

"They think you're dead," she said. "They think they've already won."

Ryan looked across at her, and the light caught his eyes so that they blazed silver. "That's our main advantage," he said. "The longer they think I'm gone, the greater chance we have of finding them."

On the far side of the lawn, Emma shrieked with delight as the housekeeper brought out the newest member of the Finley-Ryan family, a Labrador puppy they'd yet to name.

"She doesn't understand that he's gone," Anna said. "She'll get a shock, when she realises."

For a moment, something dangerous passed over his face. "When I find whoever murdered my father, so will they," he said, in a flat tone. "They'll pay for what they've done to my family."

He reached for her hand, and they made their way back to the house.

AUTHOR'S NOTE

Firstly, let me apologise for giving you all a shock, just then...

I'm joking, of course, because a crime writer is NEVER sorry for shocking her readers!

Cue the evil laughter

I enjoyed writing this episode of Ryan's adventures very much, and I hope that you enjoyed reading it, too. I can hardly believe this is his twenty-first outing because, for me, Ryan's character and those of his comrades still feel so fresh, with many more stories to tell. Over the past year, I've struggled with illness, which has prevented me from writing as many as usual, but they remain locked in my mind and ready to burst onto the pages of more books over the coming months and years, which feels like a great privilege and for which I remain very grateful.

As always, I thank you, the reader, for your kind support of my writing over the past few years, alongside my publishing team, my friends and family, and all who have encouraged me in this endeavour.

I have just one favour to ask of you...

Don't tell anyone about the twist at the end, will you?

LJ ROSS
MARCH 2024

DCI Ryan will return in

POISON GARDEN

A DCI RYAN MYSTERY

Turn the page for an exclusive sneak peek...

POISON GARDEN – PROLOGUE

University Halls of Residence
September 2005

Emily heard him moving around her room, dragging on pants and jeans, and then looking for his wallet and keys. She continued to lie on the bed in the foetal position, facing the wall, eyes tightly shut.

Everything hurt.

Her head throbbed, blood hammering against the optic nerve, sending waves of pain across her eyes. Her lip was cut and swollen, while her arms and breasts were bruised from rough handling. Her inner thighs were scratched and torn and—

And—

She began to cry silently, tears running down her cheeks and onto the pillow.

He wondered whether he should say something, then decided to leave her to sleep it off. *Fresher girls were all the same*, he thought, from his lofty position as a final year student.

They gave out green light signals all night long, then changed their mind when he was primed and ready to go.

Tease, he thought, with a curl of his lip.

Maybe she'd think twice about offering it up on a plate, next time.

Maybe she'd say it was 'rape', his mind whispered.

He'd put it about that she was up for it with anyone, and his mates would back him up—he'd done the same for them, plenty of times. That should pre-empt any awkward questions, if she decided to get bitchy about it.

Yes, that's what he'd do.

He cast one last look at her slim back, and decided she was one of his better conquests. Pretty, with a nice little body. He'd managed to take quite a few pictures during the night, which he could hardly wait to share with the lads.

He blew her a kiss, and let himself out.

Emily heard him whistle as he made his way along the corridor, but didn't move until she heard the distant slam of the outer door that led onto the quadrangle outside. Then, very slowly, she rolled onto her back, gasping as fresh pain rocketed through her body. She'd strained her muscles while fighting him, and there was a lump on her head, where he'd smashed her skull against the wall in the struggle. She was afraid to look at herself and see the full extent of the damage, but she didn't need to see some things to know it was bad.

The delicate area between her legs burned.

Emily forced herself to roll off the bed, where she collapsed in a heap on the floor. She stayed there for long minutes, crying without a sound, eyes streaming as she rocked her naked body back and forth. Eventually, when tears subsided, she crawled over to the sink in the corner of the room and grasped the edge of it. Dragging herself up, she leaned heavily on the porcelain and then, in an enormous act of bravery, looked at her face in the mirror.

The first thing she saw was the beginnings of a black eye, from where he'd levelled a back-handed smack and thrown her onto the bed.

The next thing she saw was the crusted scab on her upper lip, where he'd bitten her. There were further bite marks on her neck. Her hair was in disarray, and her eyes looked hollowed out and fathoms deep in misery.

Emily looked down at her body, and saw the dried blood against her thighs.

She began to shake as memories flooded in from the night before.

You want it, don't you?
How'd you like that?

A sudden wave of nausea made her violently ill, and she threw up the contents of her stomach in the sink, heaving until there was nothing left, not even bile.

Then, she grasped a flannel and began to scrub herself with soap and water, uncaring of the fresh pain it brought. If she'd had any bleach, she'd have used that, instead.

She needed to be clean.

She'd never be clean again.

Newcastle Crown Court
One year later

His Honour Judge Alan Golightly leaned forward and faced the jury of twelve men and women.

"Have you reached a decision upon which you all agree?"

The foreman stood up and nodded. "Yes, Your Honour, we have."

Emily held her parents' hands and said a quiet prayer.

"We find the defendant, Edward Delaney, not guilty."

Emily jerked once in shock, while a cheer rose up from the other side of the aisle, where Eddie's parents, their expensive legal team, and a gathering of his friends and acolytes had taken up half of the courtroom.

"I don't believe it," her father whispered, angrily. "This is a *disgrace*—" He stood up, and pointed a finger at the jurors. "You should be ashamed of yourselves!" he cried. "What if this was your daughter, eh? How would you feel *then*?"

"You will sit down or be held in contempt of court!" Golightly warned him.

"Kevin," his wife said, tremulously.

"As for *you lot* over there," he said, turning to Delaney's family. "You should be hanging your heads! If I knew what my son had done to a young woman, I wouldn't have the audacity to show my face in public!"

"You just watch your mouth or you'll get a writ for slander! It isn't Ed's fault that your girl's nothing but a little *slut*—"

Kevin saw red, and crossed the aisle before his mind even knew that his legs had moved. He landed a hard punch squarely on Delaney Senior's jaw before the court security guard had even made it halfway down the central aisle.

"*Scum*," he said, and spat on the ground beside Delaney. "You, *and* your offspring."

The guard fell upon him then, and Kevin was taken to the cells on the judge's order, following which he dismissed the court. His wife held Emily close, felt the uncontrollable trembling that had been a constant companion since her ordeal, and told herself to be strong.

She had to be.

"Come on, love," she whispered. "Let's go—"

Emily nodded, defeat etched in every line of her body.

"I won't leave here without saying my piece," Eddie's mother accosted them, as they turned to leave. "It's thanks to *girls like you*, that good, hardworking boys like *mine* have their lives ruined by false accusations—"

"Ignore her," Emily's mother said, between gritted teeth. "Come on."

But every word was a poisoned dart.

"Changing your mind in the morning isn't the same as rape!" Mrs Delaney threw at their retreating backs. "I'll be telling everyone what you are...a *liar*!"

Emily's legs threatened to give way, but somehow she continued, flanked by her mother and the tired-looking barrister who'd given the trial her best effort.

"I'm so sorry," she said, as they left the courtroom. "I wish the outcome had been different."

There was nothing else to say and so, with a heavy heart, she bade them farewell.

"I want to go home," Emily whispered. "I just want to go home."

One week later

"Emily! Dinner's on the table!" her mother called up the stairs, one hand resting on the newel post. "Emily!"

She hadn't been eating lately…well, that wasn't quite true. Emily hadn't enjoyed a proper meal since her attack, and that was over a year ago. Her slim, athletic figure had wasted away to something skeletal, and her fine bone structure was now a collection of bony angles and pale, shadowed skin. The anti-depressants had helped for a while, giving her a false appetite when she needed it most, but that particular side-effect had worn off. *Breakthrough depression,* the psychiatrist called it, when they'd taken her to see him. Emily's body had learned to override the drugs or, to put it another way, her mind was stronger than the pills.

Would Emily ever be able to begin her life again, at a new university? She was so intelligent, so *kind*, it was a tragedy that she'd been forced to drop out.

All because of him…

Her mother grasped the banister and headed upstairs, her bare feet padding softly against the carpet runner as she fought the familiar tide of anger.

It did no good to dwell on the past.

She knocked on her daughter's bedroom door and, when there was no reply, tried the handle.

It was locked.

That was highly unusual.

"Emily? Can you open the door, please?"

Still, no answer.

Her mother rattled the handle again, turning it this way and that.

"Kev? *Kev!*" she called downstairs to her husband.

"What?" he called back.

"I—I can't open Emily's door, and she's not answering!"

A creeping feeling began to crawl over her skin; a terrible, prescient knowledge of what she would find behind the plain white door.

She stepped away from it, breathing fast.

"What's wrong?" Kevin said, huffing his way upstairs.

"The door," she whispered. "It won't open."

He frowned, and she watched him repeat the steps she had taken; knocking and calling out to their daughter and then, when there was no reply, turning the handle.

They exchanged a silent look which spoke volumes.

"Stand back, love," he said, in an odd, emotionless voice. "Turn away."

"No," she said. "I won't turn away."

Kevin steeled himself, and did what no father should ever have to do. He broke into his daughter's room with a couple of hard kicks and found her lifeless body hanging there, from the light fitting in the centre of the room. He let out a long, keening sound, like an animal in torment, and rushed forward to grab her legs.

His girl.

His little girl…

"Get an ambulance!" he shouted. "For God's sake!"

But she was gone. They both knew that.

Emily was long gone.

Available to buy now!

LOVE READING?

JOIN THE CLUB...

Join the LJ Ross Book Club to connect with a thriving community of fellow book lovers! To receive a free monthly newsletter with exclusive author interviews and giveaways, sign up at www.ljrossauthor.com or follow the LJ Ross Book Club on social media:

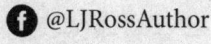 @LJRossAuthor

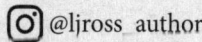 @ljross_author

ABOUT THE AUTHOR

LJ Ross is an international bestselling author known for her atmospheric mystery and thriller novels, including the DCI Ryan series which has sold over 12 million copies worldwide. Her debut novel *Holy Island* published in 2015 and reached number one in the Amazon UK and Australian digital charts. Louise has since released over thirty novels, most of which have been UK number one digital bestsellers. She is also the creator of the bestselling Dr Alexander Gregory series and the Summer Suspense series. Louise is a keen philanthropist and proud to support numerous non-profit programmes in addition to founding the Lindisfarne Prize for Crime Fiction, the Northern Photography Prize and the Northern Film Prize.

Born in Northumberland, England, she studied Law at King's College, University of London, then abroad in Florence and Paris, and worked as a lawyer before pursuing her dream to write. She lives with her family in Northumberland.

If you would like to get in touch with LJ Ross on social media, please scan the QR code below – she would love to hear from you!

Discover the international bestselling DCI Ryan series from LJ Ross

Atmospheric mysteries set amidst the spectacular landscape of the north east of England.

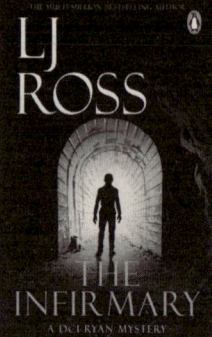

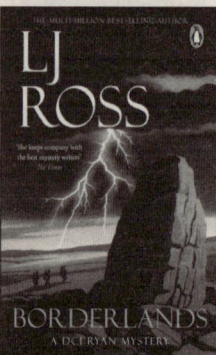

Discover the 24th novel in the DCI Ryan series...

New for 2026

If you enjoyed this book, why not try the bestselling Alexander Gregory Thrillers by LJ Ross?

Atmospheric thrillers featuring forensic psychiatrist and criminal profiler Dr Alexander Gregory. Loved by readers for the fast-moving and page-turning plots, international locations and shocking twists, with psychology adding fascinating depth to the stories.

Discover now the bestselling Summer Suspense series from LJ Ross

Suspense and mystery are peppered with romance and humour in these fast-paced thrillers set amidst the beautiful landscapes of Cornwall.